CHAMELEON

After armed men rob the building society where she works, Gemma Brent gives a televised description of one of the criminals. When Gemma's friend is shot at in the street, a forceful stranger, Carr Winterton, thinks it is a case of mistaken identity. Claiming to be with the police, he whisks Gemma away from the danger, but, too late, she realizes that he bears a striking resemblance to the gunman. There is a subtle attraction between her and Carr, but there is no way she can trust him.

Books by Jean Musson
in the Linford Romance Library:

SILK DOMINO
A DISTANT DREAM

JEAN MUSSON

CHAMELEON

Complete and Unabridged

LINFORD
Leicester

First published in Great Britain in 1991 by
Robert Hale Limited
London

First Linford Edition
published 1998
by arrangement with
Robert Hale Limited
London

British Library CIP Data

Musson, Jean
    Chameleon.—Large print ed.—
Linford romance library
1. Love stories
2. Large type books
I. Title
823.9′14 [F]

ISBN 0–7089–5246–1

Published by
F. A. Thorpe (Publishing) Ltd.
Anstey, Leicestershire

Set by Words & Graphics Ltd.
Anstey, Leicestershire
Printed and bound in Great Britain by
T. J. International Ltd., Padstow, Cornwall

This book is printed on acid-free paper

1

GEMMA'S heart gave an agonizing lurch as two short, sharp explosions rocked the rural calm of Abbeykirk's drowsy market square.

On the opposite side of the toughened glass panel in the town's one building society office, an elderly woman tut-tutted and said kindly, "Only a car backfiring, I expect, love."

Gemma's young assistant, Susan Morris, was counting out a hundred and fifty in five-pound notes for Mrs Shadwell. The girl spared a fleeting glance of frustration for her superior and raised her eyes heavenwards. Gemma smiled at the customer, but she was glad that Mrs Shadwell couldn't see how much her fingers were shaking as she laid aside the file containing computer printouts. She tried to close her mind to the events of the past week — in particular the alarm of the recent raid.

"Only to be expected that you'd be scared, dear — after what happened." Mrs Shadwell pulled a rueful face. "I saw you on the television, Mrs Brent. You're braver than I'd be, my dear; fancy you giving a description of the ruffian who robbed you like that."

"It wasn't really a description." Gemma managed a pale shadow of her usual 'customer' smile this time. Mrs Shadwell was the worst possible kind of busybody, but she had invested her money in the society for a long time now and it didn't do to rub anybody up the wrong way, Gemma had found. The old lady collected her money and reluctantly moved away, but Gemma found her gaze drawn to the window that, had it been set lower in the wall, would have enabled a view out and over Abbeykirk's market-place. Right now, though, it was steamy with condensation so it would have been impossible to make out anything at all. Some sort of commotion definitely seemed to be going on though. There were raised voices and shouts, and then the sound of a police siren.

Mrs Shadwell reached the door and pulled it open. Susan Morris and the two other cashiers were busy with three more customers. One began to argue that the computer had given him the wrong balance. Somebody's toddler was swinging on the polished wooden rail where the customers waited. He fell and set up a thin wail of protest when his mother yanked him to his feet and shook him. Mrs Shadwell's hand flew to her mouth in dismay as she peered outside. "Oh dear . . . Oh dear me . . . " The old woman's face turned ashen. "There's been an accident . . . "

Without even being aware of doing so, Gemma pushed young Susan out of the way and switched off her cash dispensing system. Susan gazed at her, terrified and speechless. "Mrs

Brent . . . " Her eyes were wide and questioning.

"If there's trouble again it will take the computer at least fifteen minutes to open up," Gemma explained swiftly. One thing was certain in her mind — she wasn't going to be caught out as she had been two days ago. Twenty-five thousand pounds, though not a vast fortune, was nevertheless enough to make her cautious.

"Lock the doors . . . " The cry came from Marion who was clattering down the stairs from the upstairs office. "It's Helen," she shrieked distractedly. "I saw it all from the top window — she only popped out for a bottle of milk for the coffee — she took your umbrella, Gem — said you wouldn't mind. Oh, God, she's been shot — I saw her fall . . . there was a man too — just like the one you described to the police the other day."

By now the whole place was in chaos. Trevor Ross, Gemma's manager, was frantically shouting orders to the other two cashiers. "Switch off the computers . . . " He strode back and forth, closing drawers, issuing commands, and at last jamming his hand hard on the alarm system linked to the local police. Customers who until then had been patiently waiting their turn, now piled across to the door, elbowing and pushing one another aside in an effort to see what had happened outside. Gemma felt her legs beginning to buckle underneath her just as they'd almost done two days ago. On Monday though, everything had happened far too quickly for her to experience any real fear until it was all over. At first she'd thought it was someone playing a joke. Youngsters of five and six often came into the office with toy guns. But the man who had faced her grimly across the counter had been no youngster — and the gun that had pointed steadily at her was not a toy. And by the time he'd given her a muffled warning not to press the panic button — 'or else' — two accomplices had joined him and were holding a dozen dazed customers against the wall. All three of the men had similar weapons, and the cold, grey eyes had stared out at her boldly from a menacing slit in the military style balaclava. That too was exactly the same as the other two men were wearing. But the man opposite her had eyes that were hard and terrifyingly calculating. His voice, though obviously heavily disguised, had left her in no doubt at all that the guns were there to be used if necessary — if not on Gemma herself, then on the customers on the other side of that glass barrier.

She shook herself now and mentally stated in her mind that lightning didn't strike the same place twice. The wailing siren of a police car screamed past the door. With it flung wide open now, Gemma caught a glimpse of her bright-red umbrella twirling crazily around the market-place in the damp, squally drizzle out there. Of Helen Blackwell, one of the mortgage consultants, there was no sign however. As people moved aside for the police car to swing onto the market-place that served as a car-park four days a week, she saw that white-coated figures were already jumping down from an ambulance, and recognized it as the nearby infirmary's flying squad force. Swiftly then they surrounded something on the ground. Gemma felt her stomach beginning to churn and promptly ignored old Mr Ross when he ordered her to stay at her desk until they knew all the details of what had happened.

"Helen's out there," she stated fiercely. "And she had my umbrella, Mr Ross . . . Obviously somebody thought it was me — Helen and I are practically the same build, and we both have dark hair . . . "

Trevor Ross paled at her words. "Oh, Mrs Brent," he murmured. "You don't really think . . . "

"I have to see if she's all right." Gemma pushed past the ambling and dithery building society manager and made for the counter door. "Drop the catch behind me," she said, taking matters into her own hands. "And I'd also lock the outer door too — just in case . . . "

"This is because of that TV appearance," Trevor Ross began. "I knew no good would come of it, Mrs Brent."

"Mr Ross!" Gemma swung round on him. "It is my opinion that there are far too many people today who back out of their obligations. And as I saw the face of the man for a fleeting second — the man who made off with twenty-five thousand pounds, then it was my duty to tell the police and alert the public . . . "

"Yes! Yes! Yes, Mrs Brent." Ross was already urging her towards the door. "I do realize that you hold very strong views, my dear. But to go in front of television cameras like that — openly inviting the ruffian to come after you . . . " He shook his head warningly. "Foolish, Mrs Brent.

Foolhardy in the extreme."

Gemma felt like shaking him. But at the same time she was only too well aware that Trevor Ross was nearing the age for retirement and had never taken a single risk in all his life. Every move he made was always painstakingly thought out well in advance. "It seemed like the right thing to do at the time," she told him steadily. "And now it also seems right that I should go out there and see if I can do anything to help Helen."

Trevor Ross sighed heavily but followed her over to the door. "The police are trained for these emergencies," he said firmly. "And the ambulance is there too. They all know what to do — they won't thank you for interfering."

"Mr Ross — please!" Gemma could have screamed with frustration at the slowness of his movements.

"All right, my dear. All right! But that fellow with the gun could still be out there, you know."

"He won't be if he's got any sense," she flung back over her shoulder as she hurried across the customer area and heard old Mr Ross snapping the lock on the counter behind her. The outer door was clear of customers now, for they had all flocked outside like ghouls to a gathering.

The crowd was scattered over much of the market-place and two more police cars were inching their way through the pedestrians straying onto the road. Gemma held back; it was more important she knew, for the emergency services to get through than it was for her to reach her friend. Somebody else might also have been injured in the shooting for all she knew. When at last she did manage to cross the road, she was just in time to see Helen, pale, but at least alive and conscious, being lifted into the back of the ambulance. One arm was supported in a sling, and blood was showing clearly on the white bandage beneath it. Gemma's hand flew to her lips and pressed hard there, clenched now into a tight fist. "It should have been me . . . " She didn't know if she'd actually said the words out loud or not, for her mind was only now beginning to take in fully what had happened. Reason took over as the full shock of the thing hit her. The bullets had been intended for her, she knew that now. Some sure and certain instinct told her that the gunman must have watched her leave her car on the market square that morning. At ten minutes to nine, she had parked it neatly. The man must have lain low as she ran to the office, dodging between cars and avoiding the crowds of schoolchildren. She'd have made a good target with the red umbrella up against the rain, but obviously he hadn't been able to get a proper view of her to enable him to shoot. So, she reasoned, he'd waited, patiently and persistently, until she should venture outside again. He might have had to wait until five in the afternoon — except that Helen had

11

borrowed her umbrella, and, clad in the regulation navy-blue skirt and jacket of the building society, had been mistaken for her as she had run across to the supermarket on the corner.

The ambulance weaved out of the market square now, its doors closed firmly on the injured girl. It turned in the direction of the bypass where the new hospital complex that had only been completed the previous year was situated. The crowd began to scatter. Police officers moved across the square, heading towards the building society office. Helen obviously had been able to tell them where she was from. One young constable hung back as he passed Gemma, noticing no doubt that she wore the same type of clothing as Helen had been clad in. "She'll be all right," he said kindly. "Just a flesh wound in the shoulder." He hurried on to catch up with his colleagues, and Gemma was left staring after them as the square began to clear.

★ ★ ★

"Mrs Brent? Gemma Brent?"

Startled, she came back to earth with a jarring to nerves and body alike. The man was tall; he had dark blond hair and a tense, lean face with a slight cleft in the chin. He was delving into the inside pocket of a light-grey leather jacket. It tapered over narrow hips. He was dressed inconspicuously — grey cord trousers, dark tie; the shirt that peeped out at the neck of his jacket had a faint white stripe on silver. His shoes were black — slip-on type — his hands well cared for. She noticed everything about him because during the past two days she'd taken to positively assessing everyone she'd come into contact with. He produced some kind of identification even as she watched. The photograph was sealed into a tough, plastic card — it was a good likeness. The letters 'C.I.D' fairly leaped out at her. She'd seen something of the sort on Monday

13

when she had been inundated with people from the local press, police, and radio. The television crew had displayed them too on their clothing. Her eyes focused on the man's face again. It seemed somehow familiar, but she'd seen so many strange faces lately — all matching up with photographs on bits of card — that she'd stopped taking all that much notice. "Do I know you?" she asked, frowning. "Were you with the camera crew the other day?"

"No! But I was there." His hair was well-groomed, her mind registered. She'd have remembered his hair, she was sure, if she had seen him before. It was thick and was swept forward then back in a deep wave. He said quietly: "I think the man who just shot your friend had someone else in mind, don't you? You're both the same height, though close up your hair has a softer texture and your eyes are cat-green — not blue like the other girl's."

"You're with the police?" Her eyes widened.

He took her arm and led her towards a large white car that was parked between several others but quite near at hand. He looked round almost furtively. "Look," he said seriously, "would you mind sitting inside? I don't think it's such a good idea for you to be standing out in the open in full view of everybody — especially as you're wearing that very conspicuous outfit."

"Hell! I never realized." Gemma gulped quickly. "You don't honestly think he's still around, do you?"

"I'd rather not take any chances." He smiled and there was half-hidden frank amusement in the grey eyes that were watching her closely, assessing her trim slenderness too, she noted with a shock.

"I think I should get back to work," she replied firmly.

"You'll be dragged into a whole lot of explanations if you do," he said lightly. "Inspector Franklyn has just disappeared inside with your manager, Mr Ross. Doesn't a quiet coffee somewhere away from here appeal to you more?"

"I'd like to follow Helen and make sure she's okay," Gemma stated with a tiny, worried frown.

"Then no doubt there's a coffee-machine at the hospital," he said. "That's if you don't mind drinking from plastic cups."

"I — really — I can't." Gemma held back, though there was no need for haste, she knew. Trevor Ross would probably assume that she'd jumped in her car anyway and followed the ambulance. And this man here obviously knew her boss as well as the police inspector by name.

"I'd feel happier if you would sit in the car, at least," he persuaded, and promptly held open the passenger door. "Just get inside, there's a good girl." He grinned to soften the forcefulness of his tone. "Look — we're both a pair of sitting ducks out here if that maniac does happen to be still around."

"Sorry!" Gemma chewed pensively

16

on her lip, but slid into the seat he indicated, warily glancing around at the other parked cars and the people aimlessly crossing the square. Any one of them might be concealing a weapon, she knew. She shivered and eased down into the seat, her fingers already fidgeting with the collar of her jacket, trying to conceal with her hand the bright little house motif that was the company's logo. He went round and opened the driver-seat door, then sat beside her and slammed it firmly shut as he had done her own.

"If he's still around, he'll be watching the building society, I'd think," he said in a completely logical tone of voice. "So maybe you shouldn't go back there for a while. Everybody in the place could be in danger if you do."

"You think I should go home?" Gemma stared at him in uncertainty.

"There were three of them on Monday," he reminded her. "One of them could be assigned to watching your flat."

Gemma's stomach felt like turning itself inside out. "Surely you don't think anybody would kill me — not for the sake of twenty-five thousand pounds."

"It was a cover," he said coolly. "The robbery here on Monday was designed to draw all the patrol cars to this area whilst they held up a major bank on the outskirts of Lancaster. Didn't you read about it? A cashier was shot. He's in intensive care — somebody could be facing a murder charge." He paused as if to let the words sink in thoroughly. "Don't you see? You could possibly identify one of them — they must be pretty desperate to silence you."

"The two robberies were connected?" This was something Gemma had been unaware of.

His head inclined in agreement. "Inspector Franklyn's of the opinion that it was all carefully planned and the work of six men in all. The bank robbery took place just eight minutes after the one here. That meant that at least five patrol cars had been alerted to dash to Abbeykirk. Three men held up the bank and got away with over a million, while those other three held you up for peanuts. The only thing that went wrong was that ruffian's mask slipping and you seeing his face."

"But I hardly saw anything at all," Gemma said candidly. "Except that he was clean-shaven and there was just a glimpse of fairish hair under the balaclava. I don't think I could possibly identify him from that. The only other thing I noticed was that he had grey eyes but his eyes were visible for everybody to see."

"But you are still the only person who saw more than his eyes," he insisted. "That's why you have to be kept safe."

"Be kept . . . " Alarmed, her gaze flew to the man at her side. "You're not arresting me by any chance, are you?"

He laughed softly and the sound held some comfort for her. "No, Mrs Brent," he replied mildly. "I'm not arresting you. But I do think you'd be well advised to let me take you somewhere safer than Abbeykirk market square."

"A police cell?" she asked warily.

"Good grief, no."

Gemma sank back against the comfortable seat. "Thank heaven for that." It was reassuring, she found, having someone willing to take care of her. "What do you suggest?"

He fastened his seat-belt unhurriedly and asked her to do the same. "Coffee first, I think," he said with imperturbable laziness in his smile. "Coffee in plastic, hospital cups."

"How do I know I can trust you?" Broodingly she halted in the task of clipping the seat-belt.

"I showed you identification — remember?" He, too, paused before inserting the key in the ignition. "And I don't have a gun — you can search the car — and me too, if you like."

Suddenly Gemma felt like a prize fool for appearing so suspicious. He was only trying to help, she reasoned, and she supposed he had the necessary authority to whisk her off behind bars if he really felt like it. From his knowledge of the raids — and the police inspector's name — it was obvious he was one of the team. "Okay — I'll believe you, Mr . . . " She stopped, realizing that she didn't even know his name.

"Winterton," he said shortly, and started up the engine. "Carr Winterton," he went on. "It was all there on my ID card — didn't you read it properly?"

"I — I suppose I was still dazed from what had happened to Helen," she confessed. "And anyway, I'm one of those people who take others on trust." She smiled and went on almost without thinking, "Keith used to say I'd land myself in trouble one day . . . " She bit hard on her lip and stared out through the windscreen.

"Keith?" he questioned politely, but his attention was fixed on the road now as he pulled out into trafffic, and he seemed not to be particularly interested

21

in any reply she might have made.

"Didn't Inspector Franklyn give you all the details about my murky past?" she joked.

"It's your future I'm more interested in," he said easily. "I intend making sure you have one."

"Keith was my husband."

"Was?" He spared her the briefest glance.

"It was a case of marrying in haste . . ."

"And taking the easy way out," he retorted sharply, and there was a note of censure in his voice, almost as if he were old-fashioned and didn't believe in divorce.

"We had nothing in common," she replied airily, omitting to mention that Keith had found somebody else more attractive. There was no disguising the note of bitterness in her voice however.

"I see!"

She was on her guard again now. "You have to put these things behind you," she replied objectively.

"Do you?" He glanced at her again. "You live alone then? Nobody to miss you if you're away for a while?"

At last she was shaken out of her complacency. "I can't be away for long, Mr Winterton. I thought you were just talking about taking me for a coffee — and to see Helen — just until that guy gets tired of waiting around for me on Abbeykirk market-place."

"Take it easy," he soothed.

"No, I won't take it easy," she stated vehemently. "I think I'd rather go home, please. I have no money on me — and only the clothing I stand up in — and with this damned logo . . ." Her hand flew to her collar again. "As you said yourself, Mr Winterton — I'm a sitting duck."

"We'll talk about it later — over coffee," he said.

"We'll talk about it right now," she replied, and her voice was icy calm.

They were out on the bypass now and following the route the ambulance would have taken. Gemma could see the flat-topped new and impressive hospital building just coming into view. But Carr Winterton never slowed the pace as they drew nearer.

"Shouldn't you be slowing down? Getting into the left-hand lane?" she asked with cold politeness.

"I want to put some space between us and that black car behind us," he said, frowning. "It pulled off Abbeykirk market-place just two minutes after we did and it's been following ever since."

Fear caught in Gemma's throat. "You . . . you think it might be . . . " She twisted round in her seat, attempting to look behind.

"Can't be too careful," he said. "There's no sense luring him into a crowded hospital though. I should be able to shake him off a few miles on, I'd think."

"But . . . he might shoot at your tyres," she began in panic. "And if he does . . . and at this speed on a wet road . . . "

"We're both dead ducks," he said cheerfully.

"I wish you wouldn't keep saying that," Gemma cried unhappily. "It makes me nervous."

"In this downpour he won't be able to see far enough ahead to burst a tyre with a single bullet," he comforted. "He'd lose control of his own vehicle if he even tried."

"Perhaps he has someone with him — a marksman or something . . . "

"You've been watching too much 'Dirty Harry' and 'Death Wish,'" he replied nonchalantly. "Anyway — if he was such a good shot, your friend would now be . . . "

Gemma shuddered. "Don't say it!" She threw him a despairing glance. "Don't even mention ducks again."

"I was going to say she'd now be more seriously injured than she actually is," he said soothingly.

"You surprise me, Mr Winterton." Gemma's voice was dry.

"Call me Carr," he said. "I've a

feeling we're going to be spending a lot of time together — and not in the most formal of circumstances."

"Where are we going?" Gemma tried to forget for the moment that they were being followed. She took comfort from the fact that Carr Winterton seemed to be a competent enough driver — if a fast one.

"Ask me in another ten minutes," he said, glancing in the rear mirror. "It all depends upon where and when I manage to lose our friend back there."

"What alternatives do we have?" she wanted to know. "Surely I have the right to know where I'll finish up at the end of the day."

"At the moment," he hedged, "the odds are on a rather seedy little boarding-house on the edge of the Lakes. How does that sound?"

"Oh, I'm a sucker for seedy little boarding-houses," Gemma replied grimly. "Providing of course that I have my own bedroom."

"Is that so?" He sounded as if he wanted to laugh but didn't know quite whether she was joking or not.

She took another quick look behind. Another car had come between their own and the one he'd mentioned. "Maybe he isn't following us." She turned all her attention to the man by her side. "Why don't you pull over and see if he passes?"

"And if he doesn't?" Dark, attractive brows rose questioningly, and he left the rest to her imagination.

She grimaced. "At least we'd know."

"When he started shooting?"

Gemma chewed on her lip again. "You have a point, I suppose," she admitted. "But it would bring him out into the open, wouldn't it? Call his bluff?"

"People with guns don't usually bluff, I've found," he said calmly. "And as I don't have one to fight back with . . . "

"He might listen to reason — after all, I could tell him I didn't actually see that man the other day."

"If he's not wearing a slit-eyed balaclava, you'd tell him that to his face, would you?"

Gemma's cheeks flamed. "I — I didn't think of that . . . "

"I'll try and lose him on the double island up ahead," Carr Winterton said thoughtfully, an obdurate little smile playing about the corners of that decisive mouth. Gemma had the feeling he was enjoying the chase. "Sit tight and hold on," he warned. "Because I'll move into the wrong lane — deliberately, and I'll have to cross over two others then if this plan of mine is going to work out."

"It's a busy island," she reminded. "There'll be lots of trucks coming off the industrial units just there."

"That, my sweet, is what I'm relying upon," he said good-humouredly.

"Then I think I'll shut my eyes," she said rather nervously.

"You do that." He gave a taut little laugh.

* * *

The end of the carriageway loomed up ahead. Plenty of warnings were given as to which lane led where. Carr Winterton drove steadily in the nearside one. "I want him to think we're heading for Kendal," he said conversationally.

"But you did say we'd be heading for the Lakes," she answered uneasily.

"You know that — and so do I," he responded with a grin.

"And now the other guy knows it too!"

"Precisely!" There was a gleam of satisfaction in his eyes. He glanced in the mirror again. "He's taken the bait," he said softly. "He's following right behind us again, but he's so muffled up in some sort of scarf that I can hardly see his face at all." He eased off the accelerator, positioning the car now only slightly in front of an enormous double-trailer truck that was in the lane to his right.

"You — you're not thinking of crossing in the path of that thing, are you?" Gemma asked hesitantly, already gripping hold of the seat on either side of her body.

"Just close your eyes," he suggested, and drove for all the world as if he fully intended taking the left-hand road to the Lakes.

They hit the first island simultaneously with the truck. The car slowed fractionally, then, without warning, Carr Winterton accelerated viciously, swinging out into the path of the truck. Too heavy to stop, the enormous vehicle lumbered on, its brakes screaming, horn blasting. Gemma caught the briefest glimpse of the black car veering away from them; it wasn't all black, she noted through her panic. It had a huge painted front of orange flames licking up towards the windscreen. She'd seen several like it before — it seemed to be a craze of some of the youngsters nowadays to pattern their cars with transfers. She couldn't seriously believe in that moment that anyone wishing to retain their anonymity would drive around in such a car. It was gone in a second and pandemonium surrounded them as traffic seemed to be coming at them from all directions. It was then that Gemma screwed up her eyes tightly, slid down in her seat and began to pray for all she was worth.

2

THE World didn't crush in on her as she'd expected it would. Giant wheels did not rip right through the car. All that did happen was that she was thrown sideways a little crazily, but her seat-belt held tight. She felt the weaving motion of the car and was still too scared to open her eyes. But at last it seemed that they were safe and right round both islands. When she did dare to peep out, she saw that all road signs were directing them south instead of north to Lakeland.

"I thought we were going the other way." She tried to keep the alarm out of her voice.

"There's another turn in about half a mile." He grinned at her again and seemed completely unshaken by what had just happened. "It will take us as far as the motorway. We can cross over it and pick up the Whitbarrow Scar road across country."

"You seem to know your way around."

"I should. I've known this area since childhood."

"And the other car?" she asked.

"Will think I was fooling him all the time and I'm now heading south."

"Do you always think in such a devious fashion, Mr Winterton?" she asked.

"Only when my life depends upon it," he replied cheerfully.

★ ★ ★

They'd covered about thirty miles when he pulled the car off the road and round the back of a large and flashy new-style inn with lots of glass frontage and umbrella'd tables outside.

"What's wrong?" Gemma asked, her heart leaping as she imagined that the other car might have come into his view again.

"Food!" he stated practically, and his lips quirked, then immediately straightened out again. "It's well past lunchtime and this looked like a convenient place to stop. My car won't be seen easily from the road — not that I think he's within fifty miles of us. Probably he's hightailing it down the motorway. It's my guess he's wondering whether we've turned off for Manchester or else gone straight on to West Yorkshire."

"On the other hand," Gemma stated, "he might be as calculating as you are yourself. He could be right on our tail."

"I'd thought of that too." He halted the car in a convenient spot, then deliberately turned to look full at her. "I just didn't want to worry you."

"Are we going to sit here and wait for him?" Her dark, winged brows rose inquiringly.

He considered her for several seconds, taking special note of the green-flecked eyes that stared out at him from the almond-shaped face. Gemma wished she was wearing anything except the drab and ordinary navy-blue uniform that did nothing at all for her complexion, or the natural wavy russet hair. He seemed to be weighing her up. She was glad for some reason that she was wearing her favourite perfume that day. "We're going inside," he told her firmly, seeming to drag his gaze away with difficulty. "So unhitch that seat-belt and we'll slip in by the side door."

There was nothing for it but to obey the man, Gemma realized, though to her own mind food was a secondary consideration to staying alive. However, this Carr Winterton must know what he was about — and it had to be said, he'd kept her safe so far — if screaming across the path of a fifty-ton truck could be called safe.

He made no attempt to touch her as they walked over to the building together. She liked that. Gemma hated men who acted as if they owned her with a proprietorial hand on the arm, though she was no militant feminist. She was decidedly jittery however as they sat down and he handed her a menu, and her gaze was drawn constantly to the window that overlooked the road they had just driven down. She insisted that she wasn't hungry. Carr Winterton had other ideas. He ordered for her when she protested that she wouldn't be able to eat a thing. He was remarkably calm for somebody who was fleeing a would-be killer, she decided, and sudden fear leaped inside her. Could it be he was too calm?

"You don't have to keep watching the road," he said kindly. "Just let me do the worrying, will you?"

"How can I?" For a moment her guard was down. "I don't even know you . . . " She caught sight of a hard gleam in the grey eyes opposite and instantly recalled the hold-up two days ago. The man who had threatened her with the gun had also had grey eyes.

Suddenly she was scared.

"You don't need to know me. Just trust me," he said.

Gemma forced herself to stay calm somehow. It wasn't easy.

"What'll you drink?"

"Straight orange," she heard herself reply.

In minutes he was back from the bar, placing the drink before her. For himself he'd brought a small bottle of Perrier and an empty glass. She was happy he wasn't on alcohol; it was comforting at least to know that should there be any more car chases, he'd have his wits about him.

"I ought to ring Mr Ross," she began, wondering also if she ought to phone the police as well.

"Later!" He sat down opposite her and conveniently blocked her escape route.

Gemma took a sip from the stemmed glass and tried to take stock of him without apparently doing so. His hair was a rich, mid-wheat colour. In her mind she tried to recall the hair of the man across the counter from her when the mask had slipped slightly. Carr Winterton didn't look like a bank robber, she tried to convince herself. No doubt though there were some good-looking ones in the world, and plausible too. Trying not to let his looks get in the way of her reasoning, she had to admit that she wouldn't have expected someone of his obvious sensibility to be all bad. It was difficult trying to blot out the physical though. His eyes held laughter. The firm mouth could be gentle . . . Quickly she averted her own eyes to look out through the window again. The road was quite a busy one considering they had left the major one behind.

The meal arrived and it looked appetizing. Quiche, cheese salad and a home-baked roll made Gemma feel hungry despite her earlier protestations. He smiled at her across the table but didn't speak again until they had finished eating. Then he asked pleasantly: "Coffee?"

Tremulously and trying hard to fight down a rising panic at the thought of setting off with this stranger again, she met his gaze. "Don't you think we should be getting back to Abbeykirk?" she replied steadily.

"I don't think that would be such a good idea," he said with a quiet confidence.

"You can't make me come with you." The note of hysteria must be apparent in her voice; she made a conscious effort to appear calm.

"No," he said softly. "But you'd be well advised to do as I say."

Did the words hold a note of warning? If so, his face did not echo it. He was just as he'd always been that morning — cool, calm and patient. She guessed he was a man who would use logic, not force. Persuasion not brutality. But he could be a murderer!

She had to go along with him. "Where are you taking me?" she asked, not budging one inch from her seat and hoping that her firm attitude would make it known to him that she was no easy push-over.

"I think Windermere will be as good a place as any," he replied.

"But it will be crowded," she objected. "I've been there before at the beginning of October . . . "

"In crowds lies your safety," he said with an easy practicality. "I know someone there too — someone who will take us in for a night. I won't be happy until you're out of that giveaway uniform."

Startled, her hand flew to the conspicuous logo again. Inwardly she cursed the designer of such a glaring and obvious little white, yellow and green house. "I'd forgotten," she said self-consciously. "But I haven't any money for clothes — I didn't even bring my handbag."

"No matter," he soothed, but his words only served to remind her that she was completely at his mercy. How could she leave him now? There was no way she was going to get back to Abbeykirk without cash. She considered causing a commotion. She wondered if the proprietor would ring for the police if she did. Carr Winterton would be well away before they arrived if she did, she knew. And she didn't really have any grounds for distrusting him or suspecting him of anything either. She had come with him of her own accord . . . and there had been that other man — the man in the car with the painted flames . . .

"I'll meet you out in the car," she muttered, pushing back her chair. "I have to go to the ladies' room."

He inclined the fair head. "I'll be waiting."

★ ★ ★

Windermere, as she had predicted, was spilling over with late holidaymakers, all out for a last glimpse of the Lakes before winter set in. To Gemma's mind they missed all the best of Lakeland's spectacular beauty by not coming in the wintertime though. She recalled the bitter-sweet time she'd been here with Keith. Her heart gave a tiny tug of poignancy, for they'd had a February wedding and had honeymooned at a little hotel near Grasmere . . . Angrily she pushed those memories away, though she couldn't help wondering if he'd taken Wendy there, after the divorce. She forced her mind back to the present. She was surprised when Carr Winterton drove straight through the town, then turned left and back into a maze of streets that must run parallel with the shopping centre.

"So — where's the seedy boarding-house?" she asked accusingly, thinking back to his earlier words.

"I didn't intend coming here," he told her easily. "I'd fixed on a place a bit more remote than Windermere. Then I remembered the clothes problem and decided it was top priority to take you somewhere we could remedy that first."

"I don't know if you've noticed," she said sourly, "but we happen to have passed by all the shops."

"I told you — there's someone I know here," he replied unperturbed. "She'll be able to fix you up."

"If you think I'm going to wear somebody else's clothing . . . " she began heatedly, but Carr Winterton broke in, and the tone of his voice left her in no doubt that most definitely he'd button her into this unknown woman's clothes by force if he had to. "You'll do as I say, Gemma!"

It was the first time he'd spoken sternly to her and she just sat and stared at him hard, all her doubts about him rushing back. Just for a moment there, that lean, good-looking face had tightened; the jawline had become inflexible. Even Keith, in their worst moments together, had never used that tone with her. But Keith had always been too easy-going . . . he would never argue — just shrug complacently and turn away . . .

She swallowed nervously and glanced at the features of the man beside her again. His brows were drawn together, the grey eyes unsmiling. "Your life might depend upon your obeying me," he stated with meaning. "And while we're here in Windermere, it won't just be YOUR life — it will also be the girl's we're going to stay with." For a moment only he took his glance off the road to fix it steadily on her face. "She happens to be someone who matters a great deal to me," he finished.

Gemma recoiled, suddenly wary. Those eyes had reminded her once again of that other man — the gunman with the grey eyes and light hair — the man who had pointed a gun at her and never wavered in his intent. It couldn't be. It must not be. Yet for the fraction of a second she had remembered eyes that had stared boldly out at her from behind the mask of a khaki balaclava just two days ago. Her heart began to thump so loudly that she was afraid he would hear it. He was pulling slowly into a gateway now, and beyond, a walled yard.

"This is it!" His tone was no longer unfriendly.

Gemma tried to sink through the seat. "I — I don't think this is such a good idea after all," she said firmly.

"Tess is expecting us," he said. "I rang her from the place where we had lunch and told her to expect us."

"Does everybody jump just because you tell them to?" she asked scathingly.

"Most of the time," he replied, and his eyes weren't hostile, but they were still cool and assessing.

He wasn't going to fool her! Gemma decided upon that, there and then. He might well be the man who had held up the building society, but she wasn't going to let him guess that she suspected. She flashed him a brilliant smile. If he could play the chameleon, so could she. "Well, let's see how this irresistible charm of yours works then, shall we?" she asked pleasantly, promptly clicking herself out of the seat-belt and swinging her long legs round as she pushed open the door.

Within minutes he was escorting her up a flight of four stone steps to a door where all the paintwork was sombre black with just a white, narrow edging round its panels. He rang a doorbell; it had a pleasant chime. Gemma heard footsteps and then the door opened almost immediately.

She was a youngish woman. No more than thirty anyway. She was striking, with red hair caught casually back and high on her head with a string of black ribbon. She was tall and slender, and had cluster gold earrings and masses of gold chain around her long, creamy neck. Identical bracelets jangled on her wrists. She wore lots of rings on tapered hands that had coral, immaculately manicured nails. Gemma wondered how she managed to match the colour so perfectly to the tight pants she was wearing.

"Carr! Darling!" She seemed not

to notice Gemma at all until Carr Winterton said easily, "Hi, Tess meet Gemma. Mind if we come inside to get over the pleasantries?"

The girl nodded at Gemma and said flippantly, "Any friend of Carr's is welcome here, Gemma."

Gemma muttered her thanks and something equally banal. Secretly she thought Tess to be over-effusive, as once inside she threw her arms around Carr Winterton and kissed his cheek enthusiastically, then linked her arm possessively through his. Gemma was acutely aware of her own dowdy uniform as she followed them down a narrow passage. At a door some distance along its length, Carr turned to her, and the redhead released his arm, with some reluctance it seemed. "You'll both want to stay the night, I take it?" Her eyes, sparklingly green, met up with the slaty-grey ones of the man.

Carr Winterton nodded. "If that's okay with you."

Tess swivelled her gaze round to Gemma and looked her up and down. Her eyes said what her mouth didn't as she took in the navy-blue dismal suit and the childish little logo on its collar. "Just ONE room?" she asked pointedly.

"Two!" His lips twisted into a lazy little smile. "That's if your spare isn't too much of a clutter."

Tess shrugged. "As you like — but I'm quite broadminded you know." She swung away towards a narrow staircase that was bright with fresh white paintwork and a blue and gold carpet.

Gemma resented the implication of her words and opened her mouth to object, but catching a warning glance from Carr, immediately closed it again. "Have you shut up shop?" he asked the girl conversationally as he reached out one hand to urge Gemma towards the stairs.

The coral pants hesitated, hovered on the second step, and Tess grinned impishly down at him. "I always close at one on Wednesdays," she said, as if it were something he should have known without her having to remind him of it.

Gemma held back, feeling at a disadvantage because she was now sandwiched between the pair of them. "Where exactly am I?" she hedged.

Tess shrugged smooth alabaster shoulders that were barely concealed at all by the yellow cotton top she wore. "Tess's boutique, love," she replied with a quick, brilliant grimace that passed as a smile. "You've come to the right place for a change of clothes. I've just had some new winter stuff in that will go well with your colouring."

Gemma's gaze swept round to Carr Winterton's face in dismay, but he just soothed, "Don't worry," and urged her on up the stairs. Gemma had no option then but to follow the girl.

The room Tess showed her was clean and well-furnished. Carr, it seemed, was to have the one next to it. Tess stood a little uncertainly as Gemma walked over to the tall window that overlooked the yard and the back road by which they'd entered the premises. "Would you like some tea?" she asked, gazing from one to the other.

Carr saved Gemma the trouble of a reply. "We'd love some, Tess — but I'd be eternally grateful if you could kit Gemma out with one or two changes of clothing first."

"Sure thing, Carr!" Tess dropped two sets of keys into his hand then swung away. Gemma heard her running lightly down the stairs.

To Gemma, and indeed to anyone with half an eye, it was obvious that Carr Winterton and Tess knew each other very well. She didn't understand why this knowledge should annoy her so much, but it did. "This is all a mistake, you know." She scowled at the man as she turned back from the uninspiring view from the window. She walked slowly over to the double bed and sat down heavily on its end.

"What's the matter?" he asked patiently. "Don't you like Tess?"

She lifted her eyes as he moved across the room towards her, then swiftly lowered them again as he stood looking down on her dark and somewhat unruly head. "She's okay," she muttered.

"You'll be safe here."

"Will I?" She glanced up at him meaningfully.

"Tess can be trusted," he said with a note of warmth in his voice.

"You seem to know her quite well." Why, oh why did she have to make such an innocent remark sound like some sour rebuke.

"We have a lot in common," he said drily.

"I really should ring Mr Ross . . . "

"I'll do it for you," he offered.

Gemma snapped irritably, "I can do it myself."

He watched her broodingly. "I said I would do it for you," he repeated, and there was that in his voice which stopped all argument.

A vision of the man with the gun of two days ago leaped into her mind, and again Gemma tried to compare that man with this one. Was it possible though? Could she stand them side by side, even in her imagination — or were they one and the same? At an identity parade would this one stand out? The height was the same, as were the eyes and hair. And she only had Carr Winterton's word for it that there had been anything suspicious about the driver of that other car — the one with the painted flames . . . "Why can't I speak to Mr Ross myself?" she asked quietly.

"Because you might give our whereabouts away," he observed.

"I'm not stupid, Mr Winterton . . . "

"I wasn't inferring that you were." He took a step towards her and crouched down until his face was on a level with her own. He took both her hands in his then, and she was so scared that she dare not attempt to pull away from him.

"I know this is difficult," he said more kindly, "but it's best if nobody knows where you are just at the moment."

Gemma wanted desperately to drag her hands out of his firm ones, but at the same time she needed some reassurance because she was rapidly coming round to thinking that she hadn't a friend in the world who cared what happened to her. And while one small part of her rebelled at the way he was taking charge of her life, yet another bit convinced her that she should trust him. Yet how could she? She stared at him, taking in the dark blond hair, grey eyes, and everything about him that could be the gunman. Then she sighed. "Okay — you win." Her shoulders slumped and the little green, white and yellow house motif was the only part of her that looked cheerful.

The firm lips twisted into a teasing little smile that somehow had the power to make everything inside her curl up. "Come down when you're ready," he suggested. "I'll go and make that phone call to your boss."

She nodded, not really believing that he intended making any call at all, but replied bleakly, "All right." She felt strangely abandoned when he released her hands, stood up and moved away to the door. Once there he fitted one key into the inside of the lock. Gemma watched him dully. "If you feel safer, you can lock your door tonight," he said, and she knew she had to trust him then, stranger though he was.

3

TESS met her at the bottom of the stairs. "Come through to the shop," she chirruped, waving a coral-tipped hand in the general direction of a door. It was immediately opposite them, but at the end of the passage where Gemma had first come into the building. She guessed that the boutique must front onto the main street down which they'd driven. She wished now that she had taken more note of the shops in the town, but the whole place had been teeming with tourists and her eyes had been searching for sleek black cars patterned with dancing flames, and tall fair-haired men. Now, she pushed her fears away and followed the trim, lithe figure of Tess. In seconds they emerged into a pot-pourri scented room that was obviously the shop area of Tess's boutique. Dark shadows filtered through closed blinds over the windows as shoppers milled around on the pavement outside, and the sun glinted on car windscreens as traffic roared past.

"I've left friend Winterton to put the kettle on," Tess tossed back with a cheerful grin. "He might as well help out as he'd nothing better to do. I always close shop up at midday on Wednesdays," she offered then. "With this place being such a tourist attraction, most weeks through the summer I have to stay open all weekend."

"It must keep you very busy." Gemma tried hard not to like the girl, for that proprietorial arm, linked so easily in Carr Winterton's, must surely come between her and friendship.

"It's an interest." Tess shrugged. "And I do have a girl who helps me at times. Now," she paused, one finger meditatively stroking her cheek, "where do we start with you, I wonder,

Gemma? What fabrics do you usually go for? And what are your favourite colours?"

"It doesn't really matter," Gemma replied stonily. "Really, all I need is a sweater or something instead of this all-too-conspicuous little house motif on my jacket."

"It's on your blouse too," Tess reminded her and pulled a wry face at the clothes in question. "Not noted for subtlety, are they — your employers?"

"We're expected to be proud of the logo," Gemma replied, sounding prim and prissy to her own ears. "The customers have to be able to recognize us instantly."

"Surely they do that when you're on the opposite side of a glass barrier to them?" Tess said with a short laugh, but there was no malice in the sound, and Gemma found herself secretly agreeing with the girl. "Anyway," Tess sighed and gazed round at the racks of dresses, pants and blouses, "I can't really blame Carr for wanting to see you in something more attractive, can you?"

"It isn't a matter of being attractive . . . " Gemma chewed on her lip. "Look . . . I don't know what he'd told you about me, but . . . "

"Not much, love. Just as much as I need to know," Tess sang out, promptly silencing her, and with the words she wafted over to the other side of the shop.

"I don't have any money with me."

"Don't worry. Winterton's credit is good," breezed back the reply. "Now — how about these?" Tess whirled enthusiastically with a pair of cinnamon-coloured pants on a hanger in one hand and something in beige angora, feminine and fluffy, in the other.

"Something plain will do . . . "

"Carr said to rig you out in something nice," the girl said mildly, gazing down speculatively at the garments and raising her brows then at Gemma enquiringly. "Why don't you just pop into the changing-room over there and see what you think of them?"

"I never wear trousers!"

"You should. You've got the figure for them with those long legs."

"All the same . . . "

"Oh, come on now. Trust me!" Tess was enthusiastic. "I've an eye for colour — and these things aren't just any old off-the-peg rubbish. The sweater came from Paris . . . "

"It's much too expensive . . . " Gemma was confused as she fingered the label. "Honestly — it just isn't me . . . "

"Try it." Tess pushed both garments into her hands.

"Oh . . . "

"Carr will like it."

Dismayed by the price, yet already liking the feel of the soft wool, Gemma sighed. "Oh — all right. I don't mean to be niggardly about this, but I do have to watch my finances quite closely."

"Don't we all!" Tess marched over to a fitting-room and swished back its curtain. She flicked on a light-switch. "I'll try to find something else while you see if these are okay." She hurried away without giving Gemma any further chance to reply.

The pants were a perfect fit and the fluffy, all-enveloping sweater delightfully cuddly. It had a luxurious feel about it and as Gemma stared at herself in the mirror she realized that she hadn't really cared enough about how she'd looked since Keith had walked out on her. The curtain rattled back on its runners and Tess stood there again looking approvingly at her reflection. "That's great — don't you think?" She tipped her head consideringly on one side. "I think you need beads though, something gilt." She dumped a heap of clothing on the chair beside Gemma and stalked back to the interior of the little shop. Gemma had misgivings as she heard rustlings and tinkling sounds. Tess came back and looped three long, jangling chains over her head. She studied her again, shook her head and removed one instantly. Another serious few seconds passed, then Tess took another one away. Her face brightened then. "Just the one, I think," she beamed. "You're not the gaudy type — not like me. Now . . . " She considered Gemma's feet in mock horror. "Sensible court shoes," she mused flatly. "How I hate sensible shoes. Yuk! They won't do at all."

Fitting followed fitting, with Gemma protesting all the time. In the end, she settled on three changes of clothing and a cosy turquoise quilted jacket. For the time being at least, she decided to wear the first choice of cinnamon slacks and the sweater she had already fallen in love with. Her sensible court shoes had been exchanged for a pair of flat suede pumps. Tess wielded a comb then and tamed her unruly shoulder-length hair that had been flattened by pulling on numerous garments. She seemed an expert on hairdressing too, Gemma thought, as within minutes she'd transformed her usual severe style into something much more soft and feminine. "Fuzz it out," the girl ordered crisply. "Make the most of it. This burnished copper is a marvellous shade."

"I've always looked on my hair as being just plain brown," Gemma said grudgingly.

Tess wrinkled her nose. "Plain brown it looked, love, with that unsightly navy thing you were wearing. You need creams and oranges, autumn tints, with that honey complexion.

Gemma smiled, for despite her earlier misgivings about the colourful Tess, she found that she was beginning to like her. She must have been around her own age of twenty-five too, Gemma mused, yet there was a world of difference in their attitudes. Tess was breezy and outgoing. She had been self-assured enough to kiss Carr Winterton the moment she'd seen him standing on her doorstep, and then link her hand in his arm to pull him inside. Gemma frowned then, recalling everything and envying them their easy relationship. She doubted whether she'd have ever plucked up the courage to act so on impulse with a man again. She gazed in the mirror pensively. Her hair certainly looked much better the way Tess had so easily flipped it into place. "I've never given much thought to colours," she acknowledged. "Nor my hair for that matter . . . "

"Come and pick out some underwear," Tess offered.

"I shouldn't . . . really . . . I've told you, I don't even have my handbag with me." A worried little frown pulled at her forehead.

"Carr's paying!" That seemed to settle the matter for the outrageous Tess. "So — no more excuses, okay?"

It was impossible to ignore the sparkling invitation in the girl's eyes, and when Tess pulled out a drawer of fine lingerie, Gemma realized that she really did need a change of bra and panties at least. She added up mentally, however, how much every item would cost, so that she could pay Carr Winterton back when she returned home. Probably he'd charge it to expenses anyway, she argued to herself, for the police force, or whoever it was he worked for and had put him in charge of her, would have made such allowances she was sure.

"I've never had such frivolous things." Gemma felt impelled to soften towards Tess.

"Another satisfied customer." Tess grinned impishly. "Maybe you'll become hooked on my creations, huh?"

"Maybe!" Gemma smiled. "I don't live too far away from here to visit sometimes."

Tess raised a finger to her lips warningly. "Just at the moment — I don't want to know that," she said. "If Carr thought I'd been pumping you for information, he'd be mad at me."

"But — you're a friend of his . . ."

Tess laughed merrily. "Rather more

than that," she said with a touch of wry humour.

"Oh . . ."

"I'm not going to get involved! Orders of Mr Winterton." Tess scowled with mock ferocity. "When friend Carr gets mad — he really lets rip, okay?"

"It must be a side of him I haven't yet seen," Gemma replied nervously.

"Oh, you won't see it — not until he knows you better — or until you give him cause." Tess gave a deep-throated chuckle. "And by that time you'll no doubt know how to deal with him."

Gemma suppressed a shiver of apprehension. "I — I suppose it's only natural — in his line of work . . ." she began.

"Work?" Tess was already halfway to the door leading to the living-quarters again. "Carr Winterton," she stated practically, "is a law unto himself. He enjoys his bloodthirsty pursuits; don't let him fool you that crime doesn't pay. He makes a lucrative living. Take it from me."

Bemused, Gemma opened her mouth to question Tess more closely, but the girl was already swinging away into the tiny passage. A door opened and Carr peered out at them. "This tea will be stewed to death," he reproached irately. "What in the name of heaven have you two been up to?"

"It's worth the wait, isn't it?" With a flourish, Tess pulled Gemma forward. "How's that then?"

Carr gave a low and appreciative whistle. His eyes raked over the whole of Gemma from her neat little flat pumps to the tip of her bounced hair. There was a glint of admiration in those eyes and it was a new kind of experience for Gemma — having a man look like that at her again after two years of self-imposed dowdiness. She'd almost forgotten what it was like, and it flustered her deeply. Her cheeks flamed. Carr Winterton's soft little laugh, which told her he'd noted the warm colour, disturbed her more than she liked to admit. "From Cinderella to princess in one easy lesson," he said in a teasing tone, but the admiration was still there — in the eyes that rested upon her, one brow raised slightly, and in his voice which wrapped around her like a cosy cloak.

Gemma tossed back her head and strode past him into the room. Once there, however, she was at a loss as to what to do, for it was a tiny place, just a kitchenette really, with a fixed table and benches on either side. Glazed pottery mugs were laid out on the polished pine, and a teapot hid coyly beneath a cheerful cosy that was festooned with giant strawberries and ladybirds.

"Shall I make a fresh brew?" he asked of Tess who was now in the overcrowded little room as well.

She lifted the edge of the tea-cosy and grimaced. "I'll do it!" Tess sighed. "You take Gemma into the parlour, will you? I can manage better without the clutter of you in here. It does help too," she went on with heavy sarcasm, "if you boil the kettle first, Carr darling."

He tweaked her pony-tail and Tess whirled round and delivered a hefty punch to his stomach. He pretended to cringe in agony, and Tess's laughter pealed out. "Shoo!" she ordered. "Get out of here, will you? O-U-T, Winterton. Out!"

Laughing, Carr took hold of Gemma's arm and steered her to the door. "I think we'd better do as we're told," he said, and promptly levered her out into the narrow passageway once again.

Tess's parlour was upstairs over the shop. It had pale-blue plush chairs and a grey carpet. For some reason, knowing how fond Tess was of bright and cheerful colours, Gemma was nonplussed, for this room was restful and cool and not at all in keeping with the image Tess tried to keep up.

Gemma thumped down in a chair and began to wonder about the man who was with her and his relationship with Tess. Her misgivings started all over again, for he was a mystery to her. Would a bank robber really spend so much money buying the clothes for her that he had? And was there any point in him doing that if he intended shooting her dead at the first possible opportunity? Did he have a wife, she wondered — or could he and the flamboyant Tess be something more than just friends? Gemma's mind shied away from that question and resolutely she put her imagination on 'hold' for the moment.

He walked over to the twin of her own chair and sat down looking relaxed and easy, his jacket discarded now. He must have left it down there in that tiny kitchen, she mused. "Do I have the right to tell you how nice you look?" he asked good-humouredly.

"I suppose as you've paid for all these clothes, you have some right to comment," Gemma returned with spirit.

He sighed, with exasperation, she thought. "Were you so touchy before the robbery," he asked. "Or is the guarded attitude you perpetually hide behind merely the effects of staring into the barrel of a point four-five government issue."

"I didn't know they'd found out the type of guns used in the raid," Gemma snapped back before she realized what she was saying. It was when he didn't reply immediately that she was aware of the tension between them. Of course they didn't know the type of guns used. Inspector Franklyn had told her only the day before that they had no leads on the men at all. So how had Carr Winterton found out if the police themselves hadn't? It could mean only one thing — he had first-hand information on the weapons because he had been one of the men using them. Quickly she tried to cover her mistake by adding, "Anyway, I don't get many compliments these days." But she was trembling all over and it took every ounce of control she possessed to face him calmly.

He laughed. "I should think not, in that prison garb you were wearing," he said, and he made no reference to the gun again. "The navy-blue with its sweet little house motif is hardly sexy or even flattering, is it?"

"It isn't a requirement of my job to look sexy." Green-flecked eyes stared out of the tense features at him.

"You should learn to take compliments," he said.

Gemma brought her brows firmly together in what she hoped would pass for mere intolerance to the situation, even though her heart was still thumping like a wild thing. "I want to go home," she told him.

"Impossible!" He lazed back in his chair and observed her.

She inched forward, as much on edge as he was relaxed. "Nothing is achieved by running away," she snapped.

"I disagree," he said in a most

pleasant tone. "In your case it could save your life."

Gemma pushed a restless hand through her dark hair. "If you won't take me, I'll ask Tess to help me," she warned.

He laughed softly again. "You'll be wasting your time," he challenged. "Tess will do only as much as I tell her to do."

"You're not being fair . . . "

"Don't you realize that Tess is taking one hell of a risk having you here?"

She shot a silent glance of hatred at him. "Then you can't think much of her to put her in such danger," she accused.

"On the contrary, Tess is very dear to me."

She wanted to strike out at him for his complacency, but just at that moment the door opened and Tess herself came in, laden down with a tea-tray. Carr rose with ease and settled a glass-topped table between the two chairs for her to deposit the tea-things on. There was fine bone china and a plate of shortbread that looked crumbly and appetizing. "Dinner will be at six," Tess sang out. "Is that okay for you both?"

Carr replied, "Fine!" But Gemma just nodded, and then asked, "Can I do anything to help?"

"In my kitchen, love?" Tess laughed out loud. "You've seen the miniscule size of it, haven't you? There's no way two women could work together in there without clawing each other's eyes out. Anyway," she swung away towards the door again, "I'll probably just microwave something, or else pop out for a pizza."

Carr began to lay out the cups and saucers. "There're only two," he brooded. "Aren't you having a cup too, Tess?"

"I'm going to hunt out an overnight bag I have for Gemma to take the clothing in," she offered cheerfully.

"Oh, stay and have some tea . . . please . . . " Suddenly Gemma panicked, not wanting to be alone with Carr Winterton again. Not with her new-found suspicions.

"I'll be back soon," Tess promised and airily whisked out of the room, closing the door with care behind her.

Carr Winterton began pouring tea out of a fat, round pot. "Milk?" he asked. "Sugar?"

"Just milk!" Gemma took the proffered cup from him, trying not to let him see how her hands were shaking.

She could keep nothing from him, however. He finished pouring his own tea, then perched on his seat and handed over the plate of shortbread. "No, thanks," she said primly.

"You don't have to be scared, you know," he said pointedly.

"I'm just not hungry," she hedged. "And why should I be scared?"

"You seem a bit jittery!"

"Somebody tried to kill me today, but got the wrong girl."

He nodded and stirred his tea thoughtfully. "But he isn't here," he said at last. "The gunman, I mean."

"He's probably found out by now that it wasn't me though," she surmised.

"We'll watch the regional news on TV," he replied. "Though I wouldn't think the police will have given much away."

"Maybe they'll have started a search for me." Gemma found she couldn't resist the jibe.

"They know where you are," he said quickly — was it just a shade too quickly he'd assured her?

"Did you phone Mr Ross for me?"

"Of course!" His face gave nothing away. He helped himself to a piece of shortbread, murmuring, "You should eat. Tess isn't noted for her punctuality at mealtimes — or her cookery skills."

No, Gemma thought realistically. Tess wouldn't need to find devious ways to a man's heart; the girl was attractive and glamorous enough to be swept off her feet for more personal reasons. Instantly she felt guilty. Why should she be jealous of a beautiful redhead, she pondered with a jolt. But Tess had everything — looks, personality, sex appeal — and Gemma was too down-to-earth not to know that men fell for that kind of girl — not the hard-working, dull and dowdy, building society under-manager type. Wendy had been the pretty-pretty kind, helpless, tiny, with blonde curls and a pert nose . . . Damn Wendy! Damn Tess! She wouldn't think of either of them, she vowed, and straightway the thought niggled her that it was because of Wendy — and Keith of course — that she had moved to Abbeykirk. It hadn't been easy living in the same town. Gemma remembered then how she'd asked for a transfer when her divorce had been made final. Abbeykirk had been her retreat, her refuge. It had been somewhere she could hide herself away where nobody knew about Keith. She'd been able to start a new life . . . or that was what she'd intended. It hadn't worked out like that. For a start she'd been too wary of men, and Abbeykirk itself boasted little nightlife. So she'd thrown herself into her work . . .

"I want to go home," she said again.

"You can't," he said, and this time there was a touch of impatience in his voice.

"You're being unreasonable," she flared.

"Don't try to run out on me, Gemma." The grey eyes were hard as flint.

She replaced her cup and saucer on the table, then clenched her hands tightly together. "I — I don't think I'd dare," she said, trying to make a joke of the words, but her voice quivered and gave her away.

Tess chose that precise moment to come back into the room.

After dinner — and until bedtime — they played a game of Trivia at Tess's suggestion. Gemma felt like an interloper. There was something very private, very special, between her two protagonists — each so uncritical of the other. There was a mercurial intimacy in their repartee that defied definition. Yet it was not a lover-like essence; it was more in the nature of a fondness, a comfortable closeness that they shared. Gemma envied Tess that closeness. At ten o'clock the redhead went and made hot chocolate for them all. Gemma didn't feel at all tired, but Carr suggested they have an early night as they had a good way to cover next day.

Gemma didn't dare ask where he was taking her. And suddenly it seemed as if her life were being completely taken over by the man. She hung onto the comforting thought that he had showed her an identity card — and it had most definitely had his photograph on it. What the other words had been she hadn't really bothered to read — except that she'd recognized 'C.I.D' somewhere on it. Nobody could obtain ID such as that unless they were who they claimed they were, she reasoned. Or could they?

"I'm not at all sleepy," she heard herself saying.

"Take a book to bed, love. I can loan you plenty," Tess rejoined. "Murder-mystery, perhaps?" Her laugh contained a deep growl of irony as she lifted her eyes and let them dwell on Carr Winterton's face.

His brows drew together heavily and his lips became a taut, rigid line as he replied curtly, "Don't push things too far, Tess my lovely."

"Only teasing," the girl joked lightly. "You shouldn't be so huffy. After all, you have a talent for . . . "

"Tess! Shut up, will you." His voice lashed her.

Tess drew in a deep breath and seemed about to make some remark which she then thought better of. She shrugged lightly and turned her attention back to Gemma. "I've got lots of books — you can go through them and choose whichever kind you fancy."

Gemma stared uneasily from one to

the other. What was it they shared? And why had Tess slanted that remark about murder-mystery at Carr Winterton?

She shivered suddenly and knew instinctively that sleep would evade her that night.

4

A WET west wind had sprung up by morning. Everywhere was drab and dank and leaves battered off the trees to swirl madly across the road as Carr Winterton drove out of Windermere. Looking down on the water from the east shore, Gemma saw that it was grey and choppy and nobody seemed to be braving the elements today. Usually the lake was dotted with little boats, but now only one picturesque steamer lay moored off Bowness. There were no crowds of holidaymakers queueing eagerly for a trip today. A map of the whole of Lakeland lay open on Gemma's knee. Over breakfast she'd demanded to know just where they were heading. Carr had obligingly fetched her the map from his car. He'd spread it out before her and had marked an obscure spot, some miles further north, with a black cross. That particular area seemed to Gemma to be riddled with tiny rivers, lakes and passes. There hadn't been time to question him, however, and anyway he seemed to think he'd given her enough information to be going on with. She gazed down at the map again as they left Windermere behind and began skirting Rydal Water. Grasmere was just ahead. It was a part of the country Gemma knew well. She'd been brought up on the edge of the Lakes and supposed she'd still be there now if her mother hadn't, surprisingly, remarried after being a widow for almost sixteen years. Gemma hardly remembered her father now, and it had to be said, she did get on well with her new stepfather. But she hadn't felt it to be fair on her mother to stay at home. Anyway, Keith Brent had come along by then and she and he had drifted into a relationship — and then marriage — with her hardly being aware of it. It was too late by the time she *had* realized just what a commitment marriage was, to argue that she hadn't been ready to tie herself down. Keith had been the first man in her life; she'd been flattered by his attentions and he'd convinced her they needed each other.

Gemma sighed and stared out at the rain-soaked landscape as Grasmere too was left behind. She was glad about that, even though the memories were fading now. She supposed honeymoons were like that though; once you'd experienced one, you were hardly likely to forget it.

The man at her side shot her a quick glance. "Are you all right?"

"Yes!" She gave her whole attention to the map again. The fells were criss-crossed with tiny roads, but many of them seemed to peter out into nothing in places. All the tracks and roads looked much the same and she knew a moment of unease as she stared out of the window again and couldn't seem to match up any of the country out there with what was on the map. "Where are we?" she wanted to know.

He slowed the speed of the car slightly and his gaze flicked down to the page on her knee. "About there — give or take a couple of miles," he said, pointing briefly to the winding line of a road that cut across a vast emptiness. The little black cross he had marked earlier seemed nearer now. At least, Gemma thought with relief, it didn't appear that he'd lied about their ultimate destination.

"Is there really any need for this?" Her face showed strain.

"I explained yesterday," he said patiently and stealing a quick glance at her again. "Don't worry," he soothed, "I haven't seen any black cars around today."

Anxiously she studied his profile. His brows were pulled together as if he might be under strain. He handled the car well, she had to admit. All the same, Gemma was suddenly overcome with nervousness as she realized she didn't really know him well enough to be alone with him at all. In Windermere it had been different, for Tess had been there — a kind of up-to-date chaperone. Though of Tess she knew next to nothing. Carr had merely informed her that it was enough to know the girl's name — there was no need for her to be brought into *their* troubles.

"*My* troubles!" Gemma had snapped, but he'd just looked at her with those cool grey eyes and informed her calmly, "*I* chose to share them with you," and Tess had come back into the room so they hadn't been able to pursue the argument.

"There isn't much trafffic," Gemma was quick to point out now, and it was true, they hadn't passed another vehicle in miles. The slated white houses that had seemed so prolific only half an hour ago had also mostly disappeared.

"It is a bit remote, isn't it?" He smiled at her and Gemma knew she shouldn't be scared; but she was!

"Yesterday you made it sound as if

we'd just be driving out of Abbeykirk for a quick cup of coffee," she accused.

"That was before I saw the car following us," he reminded her.

"All the same . . . " She paused and bit pensively on her lip. "It all seems to have got a bit out of hand, don't you think?"

Cool grey eyes pierced what was left of her composure. "At least the scenery's acceptable," he said and his gaze travelled over her, not the rolling hills and fells outside the fast-moving car. She tried to ignore the admiration in those eyes. This was not the time to be knocked off her feet by some hard-headed, tough, yet thoroughly believable smoothie. Good-looking he might be, but he could be dangerous, she reasoned.

Her heart began to thud in an uneasy manner. "You don't seem to be taking any of this very seriously," she said a little breathlessly.

"Keeping you safe is all that matters," he replied with a little shrug, and then he gave all his attention to the road again.

They were climbing steeply now and rain still cannonaded down. Dark, misty clouds brooded overhead and below them a stretch of water gleamed glassy and silver through the haze of the downpour. Crumbling shale had lost its fragile hold on the hillside further down, she could see. It had cascaded right down to the edge of the lake and fanned out at the bottom. Gemma was not usually alarmed by heights, but here the road was narrow and twisting, and still it climbed ever upwards. She began to fold up the map, and sat with it clutched between clenched fingers, her mind over-active and agitated. She tried not to notice the sheer drop beside her.

"Are you sure you're all right?" Concern etched the dark features of the man at her side.

She nodded, hardly daring to speak because her voice seemed to have sunk somewhere to the level of her knees.

"I — I just wish we didn't have to drive quite so fast — there's quite a drop down there."

Immediately he slowed the speed again and even though he'd only been doing a steady fifty, she knew, forty seemed much better.

"Is that better?"

She nodded and gazed straight ahead through the windscreen, then muttered ungraciously, "Yes, I suppose so."

"We'll soon be over the pass."

"And then what?" she wanted to know.

"It isn't so bad on the other side."

"Is it much further?" Her eyes swept up to meet his questioningly.

"Not far." He gave nothing away.

"It — it didn't look like a town or anything — on the map, I mean," she said lamely.

He flashed her a tiny sideways smile. "It isn't a town — or anything," he said solemnly.

"An hotel?" Uneasily she watched his face for any telltale lie to be revealed.

"Out in the middle of nowhere?" she asked.

"A farmhouse!"

Gemma drew in her breath, then relaxed a little. At least a farm would mean there were other people around, she realized. There'd be animals to tend, maybe milk to be collected. She settled herself down in her seat, more easy in her mind now. The man with the gun would never find her on some remote farm in the Cumbrian countryside. But then she felt a quiver of unease again, because, despite everything, that man could be the one sitting beside her right now.

★ ★ ★

The road zigzagged down crazy little ridges on the other side of the crag. Low cloud drifted and obscured much except the ribbon of road cutting into the hillside in front of them. The rain was lighter now. Gemma huddled herself into the cosy turquoise jacket that Tess had convinced her she couldn't do without. She stared out of the side window, wondering all the while about the farmhouse he'd mentioned. It didn't look at all like farming country out there, yet as they neared the valley floor she could just make out clusters of trees hugging the road further on. The land was gentle now and not so bleak and stony as before. Gradually the road began to widen out too, though in no way did it reach mammoth proportions. At least there must be something at the end of it, she mused, for at times a car or truck passed them coming from the opposite direction. She'd stopped watching for the black car now, because her mind was becoming fully convinced that Carr Winterton was a cold-blooded killer and she didn't stand a hope in hell of getting out of this alive. In the distance now was a church spire, and as another bend was negotiated Gemma saw the slated grey and dull green of rooftops too. Her hopes surged.

He couldn't be a killer — not if he really was taking her back to civilization! Her mood swung haphazardly between despair and doubting of the man, to an urgent need to trust him. But just as she really began to believe in him, a tiny side-road became visible ahead of them, and he lost no time at all in pulling the car off the road they'd been travelling along for several miles, and onto the new one. After about ten minutes it turned out to be little more than a deeply-rutted track and within another ten, they were being swallowed up by stone walls that bordered fields where dark profiles of the fells loomed purple in the distance. A shimmer of water appeared just ahead between the trees.

"Not *another* lake!" she muttered irritably.

"This one must surely be the baby of them all," he said and the tyres crunched on a mixture of scree and gravel beside the water for perhaps a hundred yards in all. The track came to an abrupt end then and there was nothing to drive upon but grass that was dotted with boulders and bushes. It was then, as he slowed, then braked, that Gemma saw the house — half-hidden by a belt of trees beside the water. In summer when those trees were in full leaf, she realized the house would scarcely be visible at all from here. It had an uninterrupted view of the lake and was grey-slated with pink-washed walls. There was one upper floor, but nobody in their wildest dreams could have called it a farmhouse! "This is it," he said, turning sideways in his seat as he turned off the engine.

"You're joking!" Aghast, Gemma stared at the building.

"It's a bit run-down, I'm afraid."

"Who lives here?"

"I do!"

"You?" Her eyes widened in the stark pallor of her face and for one moment Gemma thought she would burst into hysterical laughter.

"It won't be so bad when I've finished it off," he said with a lazy little sideways smile.

"You mean . . . you actually *own* this place?"

"My own bit of peace on earth," he admitted.

"It's certainly quiet," she said in a flat voice. "You might almost say it's like the grave . . . "

"I thought you might like it." His expression was guarded.

Gemma stared straight at him. "No you didn't," she replied. "That's why you wouldn't tell me the truth about it, isn't it? You probably thought I'd take fright and leap out of the car."

"Would you have?" he asked.

"I might." Gemma tried to sound offhand. "I'm not a very adventurous sort of person."

"You took a risk appearing on that television news programme," he reminded her.

"I realize that — now!" She looked away from him and out over the water.

"Shall we go inside?"

She shuddered. "Do I have a choice?"

"Not in the long run," he admitted. "But if you're cold you could sit out here in the car while I unlock the house and light the stove."

"You're crazy if you think I'm going to stay here," she flung at him.

"Look," he said quietly. "I'll go and make things a bit more welcoming for you." His smile and his voice were both reassuring.

Her worst fears realized, Gemma unclasped her seatbelt and glared at him. She made no attempt to open her door however. Calmly, he pulled the keys out of the ignition and slipped them into his pocket, then opened the door on his side of the car and left her. He walked deliberately over to the house, not hurrying, but almost it seemed he was defying her to leap from the car and try to escape.

More than a little alarmed, but not knowing what to do for the best,

Gemma sat tight and looked at her surroundings. The little house stood about a hundred yards away from the edge of the lake. A low stone wall marked off its territory. By stretching up in her seat, Gemma could see that on the other side of the wall was a garden of sorts, but it was overgrown and nettle-infested. The whole place had an air of silent dereliction about it, though the house itself seemed solid enough. It had no crumbling brickwork or rotting window-frames that she could see from here. Carr Winterton had disappeared inside now, and that perturbed her more than she liked to admit. Was he testing her? Did he want to find out if she'd up and run if he gave her the slightest chance? Or had she given such a good impression of trusting him that he'd thought no more of it but had left her, as he'd said, to open up the house and make it more comfortable? He hadn't trusted her enough to leave her the car keys, however.

* * *

After a few moments Gemma opened her door and let herself quietly out onto the damp green grass. It seemed senseless just sitting there alone. It was much colder outside than she'd imagined it would be. She was glad of the quilted, snap-fastening jacket that reached almost to her knees. Glad too that she'd trusted Tess's judgement over the matter of her clothing, for the warm, black ski-pants topped with a russet sweat-shirt were definitely an improvement on her own navy-blue acrylic skirt and jacket. The uninspiring building society uniform was now stuffed carelessly into the bottom of the overnight case Tess had provided. Gemma closed the door of the car and the thud it made sent shock waves shuddering into the silent air. Rooks' wings beat upwards from the trees nearby. Unnerved, she clutched the jacket more closely to her body. At the water's edge two or three moorhens were splashing and diving. It was a tranquil spot, she realized, as she stood and watched them. She was beginning to understand why Carr had called it: 'My own bit of peace on earth', for now that the rooks had settled again there was a dreamlike quality about the place.

* * *

Gemma tramped over to the low building. The door of the house stood slightly ajar. Experimentally she gave it a little push and it opened even wider. "Mr Winterton . . . " She called his name softly, and then as there was no immediate response, she stepped inside. Uneasily she began to think he'd deserted her for some reason known only to himself. Inwardly she began to panic. She wouldn't like to be left alone here. Concern edged her voice as, a little more loudly, she ventured once again, "Mr Winterton . . . " and the silence wrapped around her. Then, without any warning, he was there, appearing in an open doorway at the end of the little passage from which the stairs led up. His hand rested easily on the doorframe at shoulder height. "Carr . . . " Relief flooded her voice. "Oh, you scared me . . . "

"At least the scare seems to have put us on first-name terms," he said, and he leaned there almost filling the whole space with his six feet and more of lean muscle. "I'd begun to think I would always be Mr Winterton to you."

"I — I thought something had happened . . . I thought you'd gone." Gemma felt slightly foolish now at her wild imaginings.

"I won't leave you," he promised, and the note in his voice brought a flush to her face. He smiled in such an engaging manner that she believed him instantly.

"What are you doing?" Curiosity made her move down the narrow little corridor towards him.

"Lighting the stove," he announced.

"I thought I'd leave you in the warm car until it had started to heat up. It's like an ice-box in here."

"I don't mind." She returned the smile tremulously.

"Then come into my kitchen . . . "

"Said the spider to the fly," she couldn't resist saying, and to her horror her voice spiralled to a shaky laugh.

"Wrong room," he said solemnly. "It should be parlour."

Gemma's hands tightened into bunched fists inside the pockets of her coat. "Do you have a parlour?" Could casual conversation like this go on indefinitely, she wondered?

He stood aside for her to enter the kitchen. "My 'parlour' at the moment is a glory-hole," he said pleasantly. "Just now it's home to about three hundred books — all in packing-cases, I might add, but taking up valuable space all the same."

"I'll have something to read tonight then if I can't sleep," Gemma quipped, trying to install some humour into her voice instead of the dread she was feeling at having to stay here.

"I shouldn't think you'll have much difficulty sleeping," he responded. "There isn't much to keep you awake out here."

"Except the silence!" She shivered. And you, too, her mind echoed.

"You're cold," he stated. "Are you quite sure you wouldn't prefer to wait in the car."

"I feel like one of your sitting ducks out there remember?" She pulled a rueful face.

They both laughed, although Gemma was far from happy with the situation. Carr drew a chair out from under the table. He pushed it up against a shiny black stove. "Here," he offered. "Why don't you sit down where you'll feel some of the heat. This monstrosity will be like a blast-furnace in next to no time."

"I'm all right. Really!" Gemma sat where he'd indicated however, already feeling some of the cold creeping out of her limbs. "My gran had one of these." She leaned forward and touched her hand to one of the gleaming oven doors. "Hers was pale-cream though — not black." She bit hard on her lip, wondering why on earth she was gabbling on about her gran. She supposed it was nervous reaction, for still in one far corner of her mind was the niggling suspicion that he *might* just be the man who had held the gun on her two days ago. "It was always so cosy in Gran's kitchen," she went on hurriedly, trying to make herself sound normal. "She had lots of brass . . . and beams too — just like those in here . . . " She gazed up at the low ceiling, then sighed despondently. "I'm talking too much," she stated. "And I don't usually — I don't know why I'm doing it . . . "

A tolerant kind of smile hovered on his lips when she looked up at him. "It doesn't matter," he said, and he leaned back against the table, his hands splayed out on either side of him. He had strong-looking hands, Gemma noted, not for the first time that day. His hip-length jacket was unfastened now and it fell open revealing a flat waistline and long legs that he'd crossed nonchalantly at the ankles. There was a profound self-assurance about him. "Go on," he said. "Talk all you like, Gemma. I've hardly been able to get half a dozen words out of you all day."

She wilted before him. "I — I don't know you at all." Her voice was strained. "You haven't told me one thing about yourself, you know."

"I showed you my ID." he reasoned.

"I didn't really take it in," she said miserably. "I just saw it was your photograph . . . "

He reached into his pocket again and brought out a small leather wallet. Very deliberately he handed it over to her. "Driving licence," he explained. "Is there anything else that will convince you I'm really who I say I am?"

Gemma studied it. The driving licence was real enough. "Black Gill

Croft," she read, handing the wallet back again. "Is that where we are now? Is that really the name of your house?" She looked up again, already feeling a little warmer than she had before.

His face was tense, as if it really mattered to him that she should believe him. "Yes, Gemma," he said firmly. "This is *my* home."

"It's so . . . remote!" Hesitantly she held his gaze. "I mean . . . how do you cope with your job? You're miles away from anywhere and I didn't see any telephone wire out there . . . "

"There is no telephone," he replied and turned away to attend to a control on the stove.

"But surely you need to be in touch with . . . " She took a deep breath before continuing, for something didn't seem right somehow. "I mean . . . it is your job, isn't it? You are with the C.I.D?"

Carr turned back to her and she saw he was frowning slightly. He seemed to want to say something, but couldn't quite find the right words. "What exactly did you read on the card?" he asked at last. "The ID card I showed you, Gemma?"

Gemma stared at him. "You *are* with the police, aren't you?" she asked, slightly apprehensive.

"Not exactly!" He returned to the table again and leaned there as he had before, but now there was a tenseness to him, almost as if he were poised, a lean grey bird of prey just waiting to pounce should she decide to make a dash to freedom.

Gemma's throat felt constricted. "Just what are you saying?" she asked huskily.

Reluctantly almost, he fished in his pocket again. "Maybe you should take another look," he suggested and leaned over to toss the little laminated card onto the table. "It's confession time, I guess. When you didn't notice the one significant little word yesterday, I'm afraid I let you go on believing I was something I wasn't."

Gemma saw the word then. It almost leaped out at her from the identification card. "*Visitor!*" Aghast, she swivelled her head up to look at him. And to give him due credit, Carr Winterton did look shamefaced. "You're not with the police," she challenged, feeling her backbone and legs turning to the consistency of water.

"I'm a writer," he said.

"I don't believe you!"

He shrugged eloquently but made no verbal response to her accusation.

Gemma raged at him. "I don't believe anything of this. Why should you be a visitor at my local police headquarters anyway?"

"Research!" he said flatly. "They have a black museum at Abbeykirk."

Gemma just stared at the little piece of card with Carr's photograph sealed into it. Nothing of what he'd told her made sense.

"Well, say something!" His voice sliced into her thoughts.

She flung the card back across the

table, then rose gingerly to her feet, surprised that her legs actually managed to hold her upright. "Why?" she asked dazed. "Why in the name of heaven have you brought me here?"

"My brother-in-law is John Franklyn. He's in charge of the Abbeykirk enquiry as you know," he said. "He arranged for me to visit the museum to see the weapons they've collected there. You see — I write crime novels — murder-mystery, as Tess puts it."

Gemma wanted to believe him, but the explanation seemed too easy. She shivered, though the heat from the stove was considerable now. "No!" She shook her head. "I don't believe you — it's all too simple, isn't it? You must think I was born yesterday."

"Gemma — believe me," he said carefully, and she had the feeling he was trying not to scare her. "I swear it's the truth. I just happened to be visiting the day your building society office was held up. I was driving to police headquarters with John when the news came over his radio."

"No! You weren't with him. I would have remembered you," Gemma replied adamantly.

"He dropped me off and I made my own way back to HQ," Carr explained. "They don't let you wander around there without a security pass — that's why John arranged for me to be carrying that card."

"So how did you come to know about me?" Her head tilted up aggressively.

"I saw you on television that night." His voice held admiration. "You told the whole damn country that you'd caught a glimpse of that gunman and John was full of praise for you. It didn't seem to matter to him that you could be in danger."

"You could be making all this up . . . " Gemma chewed nervously on her lip. "How do I know that you're not the man who held that gun on me?"

Carr Winterton looked at her as if she'd lost every ounce of sense she'd ever possessed. Then he clapped his hand to his forehead. "So that's why you've been so suspicious." He let his breath escape in a drawn-out sigh. "God! I'm blind," he muttered. "Tall — cleanshaven — grey eyes — light hair — *me*!"

Gemma backed away towards the only window in the place. It was a small, four-paned affair with cheerful blue and white check curtains on each side. It would afford no escape for her, she knew, but as Carr was positioned between her and the door, there'd be no way out there either. She swung round to gaze out at the unruly garden. Beyond the low stone wall was the lake and then hillsides where the air was still hazed with rain. "Take me back," she demanded in a still little voice. "You *must* take me back — I can't stay here."

"You'll be used as bait if I do that," he replied. "I can't allow that, Gemma."

"Inspector Franklyn promised I'd be safe . . . "

"Someone slipped up," he said. "And you saw what happened to your friend Helen when she was mistaken for you."

"But why have you brought me here . . . ?"

"Because that guy would have tried again when he realized he had the wrong girl."

"But why should you care about that?" she cried.

"Look, Gemma," he said. "I saw you standing there on Abbeykirk market-place when your friend had been shot. I heard you mutter something like 'it should have been me' and I knew how vulnerable you were. I just couldn't leave you like that — an easy target for some maniac to pick out." He was right behind her now, but he didn't attempt to touch her.

"Inspector Franklyn would have sent someone for me," she challenged impatiently. "He went into the building society office and Trevor Ross, my boss, knew I was outside too. You had no right to interfere."

"Maybe not," he said quietly. "But there was something crying out to me from that lonely girl out there. Up till then, remember, I'd only seen you on a TV screen. Then suddenly there you were — a very real person with thoughts and feelings and eyes that flashed cat-green sparks because the hit-man had made a mistake and hurt someone else instead of you."

"I'd never have given that description of him if I'd known Helen was going to be shot . . . "

"But it could have been you," he said with quiet resignation.

"It *should* have been me," Gemma corrected.

Suddenly his hand was on her arm and she flinched involuntarily. "Gemma," he pleaded. "I know it's a great view out there, but won't you please come back over to the stove. You're in shock!"

She whirled to face him. "And why?" she stormed. "It's because you lied to me that I'm shocked. I insist that you take me back to Abbeykirk right now."

"It isn't safe." He stood rock-still and never moved to allow her to pass him.

"I don't feel safe here," she cried in desperation.

He replied in a savage tone, "Don't you realize? You're not safe *anywhere*?" He ran the fingers of one hand restlessly through his thick blond hair and then shook his head in exasperation. "Gemma — don't you know just what a damned stupid thing it was to do giving a description of that man?"

"You keep calling him that man," she said heatedly. "But it's a description that fits you as well." She put up both hands and pushed at him. She had to get away at all costs.

But he grabbed at her hands and held her still. "It's also a description that fits almost a third of the male population of England," he grated. "Don't you see? He must think you can give a positive identification — he can't let you live, especially if that bank cashier dies of his injuries.

"You're even thinking like him," she burst out and fear flared in the eyes he'd called cat-green. Suddenly everything was getting out of hand. "Why didn't you just say all this to me on Abbeykirk market-place?" she panted as she attempted to free herself from his grasp. "If you're really telling the truth, Inspector Franklyn would have been able to authenticate your story."

"You forget," he reminded her calmly. "I only intended taking you as far as the hospital to see your friend."

"You can't fool me that the black car really was following us."

"It was just a gut feeling, Gemma." He was becoming intolerant of her outburst. He hung onto her hands as she started flailing at him, and muttered, "For God's sake, quiet down, will you?"

"Let . . . me . . . go!"

"Gemma, be reasonable." Authority was stamped on his features which to her overwrought imagination were now those of the gunman.

She braced her hands flat against the grey leather jacket. "Let me go," she yelled.

Confident of his power to subdue her, Carr Winterton tightened his grip on her wrists and hauled her up against his body. "In heaven's name, lady," he said harshly. "Don't you *ever* believe anything you're told?"

Their bodies were separated by a fraction of an inch of leather, no more. Emotions were churning inside Gemma that had nothing to do with the fact that he might be a murderer who was intent upon silencing her, however. These feelings were more clear-cut than that. This was a man — a very attractive man, she had to admit — and his lips were dangerously close to her own. A wild, unreasoning panic took hold of her as she read the intention in his eyes. His voice fell softly on her ears. "Gemma — trust me."

Her entire body was on fire and trembling. "No!"

He gazed indolently down into the widely spaced, frightened eyes. There was a cool smile on his lips and Gemma was vividly aware of every taut muscle braced against her each time she moved. She became still in that iron hold. Provoking him with the motion of her body was like touching a fuse to a time-bomb, she realized. "That's better," he breathed. "Now — are we going to be civilized, I wonder — or are you intent upon stirring up more trouble?"

"Are *we* going to be civilized?" she argued, tossing her head and glaring up at him.

"You!" he mocked softly, and there was a gleam in his eyes that warned her not to play games with him.

She lashed him scornfully with her only weapon — words. "Why don't you just kill me?"

"Your own common sense should answer that question," he reasoned.

"I think common sense deserted me on Abbeykirk market-square," she hissed.

"Before that," he retorted. "You became a target the moment you went before those TV cameras."

"I'd do it again," she flashed. "And I won't regret it when I tell them about you — and what you've done."

"Brave words," he rapped out. "But if I am that gunman, you don't seriously imagine you'll ever get the chance, do you?"

5

TENSION mounted in the room and Gemma realized she had pushed the point just a little too far. She'd shown her own hand whilst Carr had kept calm and clear-headed. But at least her fears were now out in the open. Whether or not that knowledge would help her if he called her bluff and pulled a gun, Gemma didn't know. All she realized was that things could not continue indefinitely as they had been doing. An altogether too volatile a situation had arisen, and she had not been able to stand up to the strain she'd been under. Instantly, and despite her last statement, Gemma found that she *did* regret what she had said. But it was too late to bewail the fact now.

★ ★ ★

He still held her hands tightly. He hadn't allowed her to move even an inch away from him. "So?" he said, and there was no emotion in the gaze he settled on her face. "Now that hostilities are out in the open, where do we go from here, Gemma?"

Wretchedly she wrenched her eyes away from his face and settled her gaze somewhere on the cool grey of the jacket in front of her. "You could start by telling me exactly what you're going to do with me," she retorted.

"It would serve no purpose," he declared. "You wouldn't believe me."

"I — I might . . . "

"Is it reassurance you want?" he asked.

Her chin jerked up. "I want the truth."

"But you don't recognize that even when it hits you between the eyes," he said, and with the words he dashed her hands away. Her release came with such suddenness that she almost fell sideways with the shock of it. He strode away abruptly and, his back towards her, he studied the contents of a cupboard on the opposite wall. "I think we should eat," he went on, as if none of the previous conversation had taken place. Half turning then, he asked, "Don't you?"

"I'm not hungry!" Mutinously Gemma scowled and rubbed at her wrists where he had gripped her so tightly.

"Well I am!" Carr began to take mugs and plates out of the cupboard. He walked over to the table and paid no heed to her standing there glaring at him. Gemma drew into herself. He threw a sparing glance of impatience at her. "For God's sake," he growled, observing her with both hands resting frustratedly on his hips. "Would I be offering to feed you if I intended slitting your throat?"

Her hands fluttered in a restive little gesture of uncertainty.

"Well?" He was waiting for an answer, she realized.

"I — I guess not."

"You guess correctly, Gemma," he stated. "So why don't you make yourself useful and come and help me?"

There was little point in being unco-operative, she reasoned. And however unlikely the story might seem, there was just the remotest chance that he really could be who he said he was and was only trying to protect her.

Gemma slipped her jacket off and draped it across one of the sturdy chair backs pushed up against the table. It wasn't at all cold in the room now. He let out a low sigh and muttered, "Well, thanks for the vote of confidence at last," before returning to the cupboard again.

"Shall I see to the kettle?" she asked grudgingly.

He spared her a brief glance. "Yes! You'll find tea and coffee in the cupboard over there to the right of the stove." He grinned then. "Make yourself at home," he invited.

Gemma filled the kettle with water

and planted it firmly on the hob. That done, she walked over to the cupboard he'd indicated. "What do you like to drink?" she asked, studying the contents. "Tea or coffee?"

"Coffee. You have whichever you prefer though."

"I'll have coffee too." She closed the door firmly, then snapped somewhat irritably, "My mind isn't on this at all.

"It's still trying to figure me out," he said comfortingly. "Don't worry! Time will reassure you I'm on your side."

"I wasn't worrying about *you*," Gemma returned, trying her hardest to sound unconcerned and flippant even. "And I don't have time to find out any more about you. I'm going back to Abbeykirk. I want to go back right now, damn you."

"Sorry!" He flashed her a smile that was apologetic.

"No, you're not." Gemma spooned coffee into the two mugs and scowled at his broad-shouldered back view.

"Do you like scrambled eggs?" He opened another high cupboard and looked inside.

Gemma wasn't usually prone to losing her temper but something about the easy arrogance of those leather-clad shoulders made her snap. "I've told you — I am *not* hungry," she shrieked.

He turned towards her, holding a packet of dried eggs in one hand and an old-fashioned egg-whisk in the other. "Scrambled or omeletted?" he asked shortly and distinctly. "You have a choice. Make it!"

"I've told you . . . "

"Do you *have* an egg allergy?" His voice was stern.

"No-o-o . . . "

"Do you hate eggs?" There was a steel glint in the cold grey eyes.

Gemma took a step backwards. She shook her head. The air between them was charged with static electricity. He held up one hand and shook it at her — he just happened to be holding the egg-whisk in that hand and suddenly

Gemma saw the humour in their situation. It happened at almost the same time with Carr Winterton too. He looked disdainfully at the whisk and then his eyes met up with hers and there was laughter in their depths as he growled, "Damn! I forgot to take the safety-catch off — but I'd have used it you know."

Gemma clutched at the nearest chair back and bent almost double; tears of helpless laughter cascaded down her cheeks. When she managed to resume an upright position again some seconds later it was to see him gazing ruefully at her. "Foiled again, Winterton," he groaned. "Due to that oversight, the dame's just slugged you with her two-two Magnum!" He clutched at his midriff and dropped the sealed package as he did so.

Gemma squealed out in despair. "Don't! Oh, Carr — I'll die laughing."

He grinned soberly and stood patiently before her then. "Okay, ma'am," he drawled with a mock-American accent.

"What's it to be then — scrambled or the other?"

Gemma's eyes sparkled. "Omelette," she spluttered.

"Phew!" He feigned exhaustion. "Do you always take so much persuading?" he wanted to know.

Gemma sobered instantly. "I'm sorry . . . "

He held up the whisk. "No apologies," he ordered. "I quite enjoyed it."

"You should be an actor." Gemma was more composed now and he smiled at her before bending to retrieve the dried-egg packet and tossing it onto the work surface. The kettle began to whistle and she dashed across to it, but Carr beat her to it by the fraction of a second.

"Let me do that," he said in a companionable tone. "You're not used to such a basic way of living, are you?"

"I am quite capable of making a cup of instant coffee," she informed him.

"With this kind of kettle you need

an oven glove." So saying, he reached over and unhitched one from a hook on the wall.

She snatched it from him. "I can manage," she said, brushing past him and lifting the kettle. "I told you — my gran had one of these stoves. I know how they function." Swiftly she poured boiling water into the two mugs. Carr shrugged and turned away, bringing woven mats to the table and setting out knives and forks on either side.

"Do you know how to bake bread?" he asked conversationally.

"Yes!" Gemma placed the kettle to one side.

"And cakes?"

"Those too," she assured him.

"I don't mean those minuscule fancy things they sell in bakers' shops these days," he said. "I mean *real* cakes."

"Fruit and honey? Date and walnut? Cherry? Spice?" she asked.

"Something like that."

"You expect me to cook for you?" She tilted her head and glanced across at him under her lashes as she stirred the coffee.

"It will give you something to do," he said. "It might even take your mind off your predicament while you're learning to trust me."

"Occupational therapy?" she asked briskly and pulled a face at him.

"If that's how you see it, yes!"

"I'll bake cakes if you want me to," she said, thinking it might not be such a bad idea. It would at least give her the opportunity of assessing what weapons of self-defence were available should she need them, she mused. A nice sharp carving-knife for instance, or a heavy rolling-pin under her pillow at nights, might allow for sounder sleep.

"I'm stocked up with most things," he said pleasantly. "So if you do feel like knocking something up — cakewise — feel free."

"Is that all there is to do around here?"

He lifted his shoulders as he began stirring milk-powder in with water in a glazed earthenware jug. "There's the radio," he admitted. "But not much else in the way of entertainment."

"Trivia?" she asked innocently and was rewarded with a dour grimace.

"I don't think Tess will ever forgive me for beating her last night," he said softly and with a little laugh.

"Do you have your coffee black?"

"Yes," he said. "No milk — no cream. Not that you'll find either of the fresh kind around here. It's all either tinned or powdered."

"You led me to expect a farm," Gemma reproached. "I thought there'd be eggs, and milk from the cows."

"This place was once a farmhouse," he said. "At least — that's what it says on the deeds."

"You'll have to get some chickens," she parried.

"I couldn't bear to kill them." His answer was spontaneous.

"I thought you'd be accustomed to that — killing!"

He looked her over thoughtfully.

"I don't go around killing people," he responded swiftly. "Anyway — I'd make pets of them, and pets become friends. You can't just eat your friends, can you?"

"I suppose not." Logically, Gemma observed him. "I take it we're still talking chickens and not people?"

"Right!" he said and shrugged off the leather jacket, throwing it aside carelessly onto the chair that Gemma had occupied earlier.

She sipped at her hot coffee and he joined her over at the table and picked up his own drink. A silence fell upon them that might have turned uneasy had he not spoken when he'd downed half his drink. "I suppose I'd better show you around the place before we eat," he said. "I'll light fires in some of the other rooms before nightfall too — it can turn cold later on."

Gemma took another sip of her coffee — a longer one this time. She prayed silently that there would be a guest-room. She wanted to yell at him that she had no intention of staying here, but it seemed futile somehow. If she did that, she knew he'd prove to her he could make her stay, she had no doubt of that at all.

"Don't expect too much," he warned as he walked away towards the door.

"I won't!" Resolutely she placed her own mug beside his, then followed him. From the long, dim passageway, two more doors led off. He flung one open and said, "The spider's parlour."

Gemma saw a largish room, beamed and with an old-fashioned fireplace grate and age-blackened oak mantel running the width of it. "An ingle," she said mildly. "How very cosy."

★ ★ ★

There were four large packing-cases over by the window. He nodded in that direction. "The books I told you about," he observed, leading her into the room. It was clean, she saw, and all the walls had been given a fresh coat of ivory paint. "I only finished in here last weekend," he said, and she saw that at one end of the room heavy shelving had been fastened to the wall, making one large bookcase that reached from floor to ceiling in an alcove.

"Why don't we start unpacking them this evening?" Gemma suggested, for at least with something like that to occupy them, there shouldn't be long, awkward silences. Books were complex things, she'd always found, and ever a talking-point. Besides that, she wanted to know if Carr had indeed written any books for surely amongst so many there would be at least some of his own.

"Maybe!" he replied guardedly and turned and walked out of the room.

The other door in the passageway led to a study in which was a desk of giant proportions, a chair and a free-standing bookcase. When they came out of there and moved towards the stairs, Gemma saw that this part of the house was the only bit that had floor-covering. A brown, dusty, cord carpet covered the stairs. "A legacy from the previous owner," Carr said apologetically. "I only left it down because I intend stripping this treacly varnish off the woodwork. I thought it might protect the floorboards underneath, deaden sound too — the stairs tend to creak, you'll find."

In the bedroom that was obviously his own, the furniture was of heavy mahogany. There was a double bed, wardrobe and chest of drawers to match, and on a small chest below the window a substantial oil-lamp with pale-yellow shade brought the only splash of colour to the room. Only then did Gemma realize that there was no electricity in the house. He showed her two other rooms, both sparsely furnished. One had a double bed and the other, a much smaller room, a single divan. "Take your pick," he said easily. "Whichever you choose, the bed can be made up after we've eaten."

The smaller of the two rooms was

next to Carr's bedroom. He would be near at hand should anyone break in. Immediately Gemma replied, "I'll take the small one."

"You can knock on the wall if you want me," he said, almost as if he'd read her mind.

Gemma tossed back her head and replied flippantly. "The man in the black car might just turn up."

"Quite!" he said softly, and his glance flicked over her. She wondered tremblingly if her words had fooled him into thinking she believed him about the gunman in the car. But then she knew instinctively that no-one could fool Carr Winterton, he was much too astute for that. "Let me show you the bathroom," he continued. "But for goodness sake, don't laugh, will you?"

At the farthest end of the small landing, the bath-cum-toilet was tucked away. Its plumbing was ancient — the tall cistern could have been straight out of a museum. There was a long swing chain with mother-of-pearl handle. The bath itself was huge and made of cast-iron. It had splayed-out feet with curled claws clinging to the bare wooden floor. Black, peeling paint on its outside did little to endear itself to Gemma. The inside was white enamel but discoloured with age. She managed to smother a laugh.

"Don't hurt its feelings," he hushed her. "I always have the feeling that it will leap up off the floor if I give it enough reason."

"It's like a piebald lion," she whispered.

He nodded thoughtfully. "You're right," he said. "I think it has something to do with those ungainly brass taps at the other end. They look remarkably like ears."

"And the feet . . . " Gemma began to giggle.

"The water is always hot," he said in a practical tone of voice.

"I know. My gran had a stove . . . "

"Just like mine," Carr finished in all seriousness. "Except of course that your gran's stove was pale-cream."

"I do go on a bit about my gran, don't I?"

"Does she still have the stove?"

"She died when I was eighteen."

"You must miss her," he said kindly.

They turned — both at the same time — to walk out into the corridor again. The room, however, didn't allow for two people being in there, let alone them both swinging round together. Gemma's shoulder jostled against Carr's arm. She would have leaped away, but there was nowhere to leap; she just bumped into him again.

"Steady," he said, and his hand came up to catch hold of her.

"I'm all right." Fear shrilled her voice. She stepped forward again, but the inward-opening door blocked the way.

"Just stand still," he ordered and his hand fastened around her wrist.

Gemma's heart lurched sickeningly. They were close up against each other, so close she could feel his warm breath against her forehead which just about reached his lips.

"Let me go . . . " Gemma began to panic.

"Gemma! For God's sake, don't." He was very calm. He would be, she argued, trying to make herself obey him. He couldn't know the effect that being so close to him was having, she reasoned. She made herself very still. "That's better." There was a smile in his voice. "I'll stand back," he said. "Then you can pull the door a little wider, okay?"

Gemma nodded. "Yes!" Her voice, she was horrified to hear, was all trembly.

He took a step back and propelled her in front of him. "Right — you're free of the lion's den," he said with a touch of humour.

Gemma pushed the door back and fled out into the passage. Once there she waited for him to join her. She was breathing hard. It wasn't only that she had been scared, she knew, it was just that they had been forced together in there, and it had unsettled her.

He seemed to understand and made no reference to what had happened. "If you'd like to get the feel of your bedroom, I'll fetch your clothes up from the car," he offered. "You can unpack them while I cook the meal."

"Thanks!" There was still a shaky note in her voice. She halted outside the doorway of the little room allocated to her. "I need to freshen up."

"The water will be hot — almost at boiling-point," he said. "So be careful."

The conversation was polite. Too polite, she sensed. His voice was cool, but his eyes were something else altogether. He was looking at her and it was unsettling to say the least — almost as if he'd never really noticed her until that moment when they'd been jammed together in a bathroom that housed a piebald lion . . .

Gemma cursed her over-active imagination. It hadn't meant a thing to him, she convinced herself. She lifted her chin almost defiantly. "May I have an oil-lamp, too — tonight?" she asked brightly.

His slow smile of understanding flustered her even more. "I'll light one in all the rooms when it's dusk."

She nodded. "Thank you!" There was safety in cold politeness, she reasoned.

"I can even run to a hot-water bottle," he offered.

"I might just take you up on that." She wished he would go.

"Towels, soap and anything else you might need are in the cupboard at the side of the bathroom," he informed her calmly. "So, help yourself."

"Thank you," she said again.

It was well after midday, not a scary time at all. Even a lazy, pale sun was trying to penetrate the window at the top of the stairs. Carr Winterton turned away and left her. She knew it wouldn't take him long to bring up the overnight bag she'd left in the car. Maybe she should trust him! She watched the tall figure striding away down the stairs, but in the silence of the house when he was out of her sight, Gemma couldn't quell the doubts about him that insisted on creeping back into her mind.

6

FROM somewhere close at hand there was music. Gemma's eyes flew wide open. Her alarm-clock hadn't woken her, she knew. Of course not! After sleep came remembrance. The little digital alarm was back in her cold flat at Abbeykirk, and she was here, tucked up and warm in Carr Winterton's spare bedroom in his house called Black Gill Croft. She stretched lazily and thought of the crouching piebald lion just along the passage. Last night she'd taken a hot soapy bath in it just before bedtime. It had been the most comfortable bath she'd ever taken in her life. She'd been relaxed afterwards and must have drifted off to sleep as soon as she had curled up on the narrow little divan bed. That must account for how wide-awake she felt this morning — that or else the fresher than fresh air that blew off the fells and found every single crevice in the woodwork around the window-panes. She lay still and listened for sounds of movement. The music, she guessed, would be coming from Carr's radio down in the kitchen. It ran off batteries and last night they had listened to a spooky play on Radio Four as they'd started to sort out his boxes of books in the 'spider's parlour'.

But something else apart from the music was filtering through now, something that made Gemma throw aside the covers and begin to dress hastily. She straightened her bed swiftly, then tucked the cotton nightshirt — paid for by Carr at Tess's boutique — under her pillow. Tidied now, she took stock of herself as the aroma of bacon that had finally roused her became too tantalizing to resist any longer. She whisked up her towel, brush and comb and ran along to the bathroom. That bacon could not be ignored any longer.

The news bulletin was just finishing as she reached the kitchen some six minutes later. The weatherman was forecasting a fine day, and Gemma was glad she'd guessed at that first thing and had dispensed with the fleecy sweat-shirt. This morning she'd settled for a light-gold overshirt in brushed cotton and a pair of denims. She felt rather conspicuous in jeans because she'd never worn them before. Keith used to hate women who wore trousers, she recalled. Keith, Gemma decided then and there, had been an old-fashioned fuddy-duddy — a truth she'd never have admitted before this week. Tess had argued that jeans would be warm and practical — as well as being good to look at. When Gemma saw Carr Winterton's obvious glance of approval as she entered the kitchen, she was glad she'd allowed herself to be talked into having the jeans. She walked over to the stove, wrinkling her nose.

"Sit down," he growled. "You're too late to help out."

"Your bacon is much better than an alarm-clock," she retorted brightly. "And I'm starving."

"It's the air," he said and pushed Danish rashers around in one pan, then left that alone and stirred scrambled eggs in another.

"Shall I pour the tea? Or is it coffee?"

"Tea!" he stated. "I'm definitely an Englishman at breakfast-time." He raised one brow and gave her a charming smile that melted her insides. "I take it you slept well?"

It would be small-minded not to smile back, she reasoned, and anyway, she'd done it before she realized. Then she whirled away to the table feeling utterly confused because something seemed to leap inside her, making her feel dizzy and excited and wanton. She'd forgotten just how heady a man's presence in the kitchen could be — especially first thing in the morning.

141

There was something decidedly wicked about it, as if breakfast together meant that something else had also happened — together. But how could a mere smile from a relative stranger make her experience sensations such as these? Even Keith had never aroused such emotions inside her. But Keith was different, she recalled. Keith would never have dreamed of cooking breakfast for her. No matter how late down she was, he'd still be sitting reading the newspaper and waiting for her to put the kettle on. The only conversation would revolve about the day's headlines, the price of petrol, the weather. Sometimes he'd be grouchy and would start blaming the government for everything.

* * *

The radio wasn't turned up loud. Gemma hummed to the tune it was playing. Thank goodness it wasn't pop, she thought happily. That would be too much to put up with at this early hour. This was something nostalgic from the fifties. She tried to recall the title, but hummed it all the same when she couldn't. Carr brought two plates to the table as she finished pouring the tea. "I asked you a question a couple of centuries ago," he said as he placed one of the plates in front of her and the other where his own place was.

"Yes! I slept well, Mr Winterton," she said. "And I had the most marvellous bath ever in the old lion last night."

"Eat your breakfast," he ordered, and promptly sat down opposite, looking relaxed and rugged and very much the outdoor man in a sensible black crew-neck sweater and light-beige slacks.

Gemma obeyed and ate heartily. It was decidedly satisfying, she found, having someone looking after her and taking charge. With Keith it had been so very different. He'd expected her to 'mother' him and then turn into a sex-kitten at nights. It was like being two people — or, more to the point, one person playing a continuous role. With a shock, Gemma realized that even now she wasn't absolutely sure which one he had preferred.

"You're very pensive. Is the bacon tough?"

She concentrated very hard on Carr Winterton's face. "No," she replied in all seriousness. "I was just thinking that I'd never had a man cook me breakfast before."

"I'm glad it isn't my cooking that made you frown."

"Was I frowning?"

He nodded and took a long drink of tea before replying, "More than frowning, I think."

"I was thinking about Keith."

"And?"

"Oh, nothing really."

"You can tell me."

Gemma clasped both hands around her teacup. "Can I?"

"Cross my heart. I won't tell a soul."

"You're too flippant." She scowled at him. "Aren't you ever serious?"

"Do you prefer your men serious, Gemma? Do you go for the strong, silent type?"

Her eyes flew to his face. "I'm *off* men!"

"You're scared, I think," he said, and now his tone wasn't light at all. "Why, Gemma?" he wanted to know.

Gemma was wary, but she lifted her shoulders in what she hoped was a good imitation of a nonchalant little shrug. "This is a big change for me. Until a few days ago I was settled into a dull and boring routine. Nothing exciting had ever happened to me in all my life before."

"Do you find this exciting?" he asked incredulously. "A meagre breakfast in a tumbledown house with no electricity and on the edge of nowhere."

It was exciting! Suddenly Gemma knew that it was. But the house and its location had little to do with that. It was the man himself; this man, sitting opposite her and watching her so attentively, was what made the moment magical and the place unreal. Yet even as her mind registered the fact, she forced herself to emphatically deny that she found Carr Winterton attractive. He might be the gunman, and it wasn't going to help any if she went all soft and mushy-eyed on him. "It's different," she said happily. "And it's certainly less dreary than counting out money and having to answer to a little green computer-screen for all my actions."

"I really think you're beginning to trust me." He sounded surprised.

Gemma looked up again and pushed her empty plate away. "Why shouldn't I?" she asked, bestowing her brightest smile ever on him. "The evidence is all in your favour, isn't it? I've seen your I-D and your driving licence — and this must be your house. Nobody else would want to live here, I'm sure."

"Do you like it?"

"The house?"

He inclined the blond head in a single cursory nod and the lazy grey eyes flickered to rest on her again. Gemma made a huge effort to ignore that smouldering, sexy smile even though her toes were curling up and her knees evaporating again. It could be deliberate, she told herself severely. It could be a practised art of the man — to convince her he was genuine. "It's nice," she said guardedly. "Shall I wash up the breakfast things now?"

"Nice!"

"Well — it has potential, doesn't it?" She rose to her feet in an altogether too abrupt manner and scooped up her cutlery and plate. "I can see why you were attracted to the spot, it's peaceful and it has some lovely views . . . "

"You sound as if you're trying to sell it to me," he remarked easily, but he joined her over at the deep, glazed earthenware sink where she'd begun to run hot water over the crockery.

Gemma laughed softly at his teasing tone. "I'd prefer it myself with electricity and a telephone," she said, splashing the water around and sparing only the most fleeting of glances at him.

"It's all in hand," he told her lightly. "But as the mains supply is back there at the main road, it seems I'll have to have a special line laid on. They also suggest a back-up generator in the cellar as power lines here are a bit vulnerable in wintertime."

He made it sound so plausible, just as if he really was someone entirely genuine. Gemma wanted to be taken in by his words. Why was it, she wondered, that normally she was the most trusting and unsuspecting of people? But where Carr Winterton was concerned, she seemed ever to be looking for a trait in his character that just wasn't there.

"I see," she murmured politely as she continued washing up the plates and piling them, together with the cups and saucers, on a wooden drainer beside her. She was a little surprised when Carr took a crisp, white towel from

148

a drawer and began to dry the things and put them away. "You don't have to do that," she said and her words were sharper than she'd intended them being. "I can manage . . . "

"Why should you?" His voice was warm, caring. "I want to do it. Maybe if I don't work you too hard, you'll come and visit me when the electric and telephone are laid on."

Inside, Gemma felt tied in knots. How could he talk to her like that if he intended killing her? And if that really was his purpose — to do away with her — why hadn't he carried out his plan already? She swirled water round the sink, scrubbing it clean again with the soft brush she'd been using. Then she turned to him. "Books?" she asked briskly. "Or shall I bake some bread?"

"Bread!" he stated emphatically. "I'll help if you like."

"You can't help with bread-making," Gemma replied. "It doesn't take two people to punch dough into shape."

"I'll learn if I watch," he said calmly.

"And I can clean up the bowls and tins and whatever."

"We don't have to share *all* the work," Gemma said.

"But we may as well." He moved away to another cupboard that was built into an alcove near the stove. From there he began to lift down packets of flour from a high shelf and place them on the table. "You're not tall enough to reach up here." He grinned across at her.

Gemma scowled. "I don't like anybody peering over my shoulder when I'm working."

"But I can't leave you, can I?" he reasoned.

Gemma swallowed nervously. "Surely it wouldn't matter if you were in another room . . . "

"I was on Abbeykirk market-place when your friend was shot at," he reminded her. "I was less than ten yards away from the girl."

"You were?" Wide-eyed, she stared at him.

"Like the killer — I thought she was you," he said. "I was running over from my car when she fell."

If he was so near, he could have used a gun himself, Gemma realized. But at such close quarters why hadn't he made a better job of the shooting? Maybe Helen had turned round at the last moment, she thought uneasily. Had she surprised him? And, almost too late, had he seen it was the wrong girl? He could have managed to lose himself in the crowd that had congregated and so prepare to lie in wait — this time for the *right* girl.

"I — I didn't know . . . "

"How could you?" he asked. "We didn't hang around for long discussions, did we?"

"I suppose not." Gemma walked thoughtfully over to the stove and checked on the heat, then she swung round to face him. "I'll need tins," she said, eyeing the things on the table. "Do you have baking-tins and bowls?"

He brought out everything she might need from the ceiling-high cupboard. Startled, she observed that the baking-tins were not in fact new. As if he read the question in her eyes, he attempted to explain. "My mother insisted I should have all this . . . " His hand encompassed the laden table with a careless sweep. "She filled a box with pots and pans for me, then another with what she calls 'essentials' — flour, sugar, all those things." He smiled disarmingly. "She even gave me a cookery-book, believe it or not. It must be in with the others we were unpacking last night."

"Can I see it, please?"

"Don't you believe me?"

She didn't, but she couldn't tell him that. Gemma was confused. She'd never been any good at deceit. "It's just — well, I'd like to check on oven temperatures," she stammered out. "It's a long time since I did any baking, you see."

She hadn't fooled him. She could

read it in his eyes when she dared to look at him. Again she knew the old fear, and realized she must not make him suspicious. But before she could begin making excuses or long explanations, he spoke abruptly. "Okay! You shall have the book. Come with me."

"It doesn't matter — really."

"I insist, Gemma," he said quite pleasantly, and there was a mocking undertone to the words. He held out one hand. "Come along — it shouldn't take long to find it."

"Carr! You don't have to . . . "

"Gemma!" He sighed heavily. "It's obvious you don't believe a word I've told you about my mother — but this is one thing I can prove." He gave her no time for further argument but walked round the table and took hold of her hand in his own. At once she tried to pull away. It was impossible, she knew, even before she tried it. Quite gently, but very firmly, he led her out into the passage and down to the parlour.

Once there he pushed the door shut behind them both, then released her hand. The books were exactly as they had left them the night before. He delved into the box that was already open and searched around the few that were left. Gemma's heart was thudding wildly now. She was becoming more apprehensive too. He moved on to the second box and unknotted the twine that held it. Carefully he began to lift out books, half a dozen or so at a time, placing them in neat piles on the floor. Not moving from the spot where he'd left her, Gemma watched in ever mounting dismay.

"It really didn't matter all that much," she said miserably.

"Oh, but it matters to me, Gemma my sweet," he replied, and he glanced up at her fleetingly from his crouched position by the box. There was a hint of steel in that gaze and it warned her that to protest further would be to invite trouble. The next few seconds dragged out longer than an hour would normally have done. But at last, it seemed, he found what he was looking for. He held it up for her to see for herself that it was indeed a cookery-book — and a very old one too.

Slowly she crossed the room and knelt beside him. "I'm sorry, Carr." There was the merest tremor in her voice.

He placed the book firmly in her hands. "I'm sorry, too," he murmured. "I'd just been kidding myself that you were beginning to trust me." With one finger placed just under her chin, he tilted her face towards his own. "Why, Gemma?" he wanted to know. "Why in God's name are you so suspicious?"

She shook her face away and stared down at the dusty jacket of the book. "I — I don't know," she muttered.

"It isn't just me, is it?" he said perceptively. "Was it that husband of yours who hurt you?"

Pain flashed across her face. "That's in the past," she snapped.

"Do you still love him?"

"Love?" She stared at him incredulously. "Love died a long time ago," she said. "Love ended when I found out he'd been seeing a girl half his age for six months or more. Wendy was eighteen — Keith was thirty-seven. God — I was a fool."

"So you divorced him."

"Yes."

"And you haven't seen him since?"

"I moved away," she said. "I couldn't bear to be in the same town."

"You have to forgive and forget sometime, Gemma," he said kindly.

"I'll never forgive . . . " She rose slowly to her feet.

"Or trust another man?" he asked solemnly.

"You can't blame me for not trusting you," she flashed at him.

"I'm not a killer!"

Gemma stared down at the book in her hands. "Maybe not," she said.

"So don't treat me the same way you did him — the husband."

She turned away and something fell from the pages of the book she was holding. Her eyes followed the progress of the postcard-size photograph to the floor. Carr bent down and retrieved it and his mouth set instantly into a severe line.

"She's . . . pretty . . . " Gemma felt she had to say something — anything — in order to disperse the bitterness she saw in his face. The smiling face of the girl in the photograph was vaguely familiar. Her hair was a mass of shoulder-length golden ripples, her eyes softest brown. But it was the features . . . and if her hair had been red . . . "Tess?" She couldn't stop the name tumbling from her lips.

He looked startled. "Heavens no! Debra is Tess's sister though."

"Debra?"

"My wife!" He turned away and placed the photograph on one of the piles of books. Then, he wasted no more time, but walked over to the door again. His expression left her in no doubt at all that he wasn't in the mood for questions.

* * *

Back in the kitchen, Carr seemed to have gained control over his feelings. He weighed out flour and made general conversation. To all outward appearances he was the same man she'd been talking to over breakfast that morning. Gemma was the same too — except that now she knew he had a wife — and somewhere deep down inside her, something was beginning to hurt . . .

* * *

The bread was a great success. Carr made soup out of a packet to eat with crusty rolls she'd baked for lunch. The loaves, round and floury, were set aside to cool on wire trays. In the oven an apple sponge was giving out a delicious hint of what would follow. Gemma had discovered the house had a cold store attached to the outside at the back. In it she'd found stacks of apples and some potatoes too.

Carr suddenly surprised her by saying, "I suppose a spot of keep fit wouldn't do any harm — a walk outside at least."

"Do you mean that?"

"We'll keep to the lakeside. You'll need something a bit warmer than what you're wearing though."

"My jacket?"

He nodded. "That should do."

Gemma cleared away the remains of the meal when they'd finished, and Carr again helped her. Afterwards she turned eagerly to him. "I'll need to freshen up — brush my hair to get rid of the flour from baking."

He laughed. "I'll give you ten minutes."

She nodded happily.

"I'll knock on your bedroom door if I'm ready first," he said.

"I'll come downstairs . . . "

"No, Gemma. I don't want you downstairs alone."

"Okay!" Nothing could dampen her spirits as she thought of being out in the clear fresh air again.

He dropped the catch on the front door as they went upstairs. It was a simple precaution, he said, but it made Gemma feel uneasy. "Don't look so worried," he teased as he caught up with her on the narrow little landing.

"Surely nobody could know I'm here, could they?" she asked nervously.

"No way at all," he comforted.

"Why don't I believe you?" She gazed at him, perturbed.

"It's a habit you've got into," he said easily. "We shall have to find some way of breaking it."

He was so relaxed himself that it was difficult to think there might be any real danger to her, either from the man himself or an outsider. Gemma forced a smile to her lips. "I'll try not to be long," she promised, and with the words walked quickly to her own bedroom.

★ ★ ★

There was no urgency, she knew. All the same, she hurried, and in less than five minutes was ready. The turquoise jacket was warm indoors so she didn't wait to fasten it as quietly she closed the door of her room and turned towards Carr Winterton's. His door was open, and it seemed like the most natural thing in the world to tap lightly on it and peep inside, a smile hovering on her face. But the smile froze instantly and her hand fell back to her side. Carr Winterton glanced up from the bed where he was perched and a flicker of alarm showed in his eyes. He was just loading the gun — that much was obvious to Gemma. He snapped the cartridge into place and rose to his feet — menacingly, it seemed to her over-wrought imagination. The weapon was still in his hand and that was all she saw, then her gaze rose in horrified fascination to his face — to the steady grey eyes that were looking directly at her.

She cursed herself as she turned and ran. Cursed him, too, but she had a head start on him, she realized. In no time at all she was at the bottom of the stairs and fumbling with the dropped catch on the door. Her breath cut into her lungs in deep sobs of panic. Somewhere where her heart should be was an aching void that, even as she launched herself headlong from the house, was already filling up with misery. She didn't stop to reason anything out at all. Monday morning was all she could think about. Monday morning — when a pair of grey eyes had stared out of a balaclava mask . . . There was a stitch in her side that was making her gasp. The grass was slippery beneath her feet as she headed in the direction of the main road again. At some point she passed the car, parked on a sloping bit of ground between the lake and the house. Reason told her she'd never make it, for the road must be four or five miles away towards the village that she'd seen before they turned off.

* * *

He brought her down with something resembling a rugby tackle. It shocked every ounce of breath out of her, but luckily the grass was overgrown and thick. It cushioned her fall, as did the quilted jacket, but all the same a shaft of pain shot agonizingly through her left shoulder. She keeled over onto her back and began to tear into Carr Winterton in a frenzy. Her jacket fell open, hampering her movements. Gemma belaboured him with fists and fingernails. There was no chance for words, all her efforts were concentrated on hurting him — and, ultimately, freedom. Carr fought back, but only hard enough to subdue her flailing arms and legs. Gemma had no breath left to plead with him, and anyway, this was a fight for life. All she knew was that he had a gun — and he'd told her in the car that first day that he *didn't* have one. He'd lied! And if he'd lied once, how many more times too? Slowly the battle was being brought under control as Gemma's efforts dwindled under his greater strength. But with exhaustion all but upon her, she bombarded him about the head and shoulders one last time. Her nerves hung in shreds and she could hear frantic sobs breaking from her lips as she tried to disentangle her legs from the length of tough muscle that was half lying across her and pinning her to the ground. Swiftly then he caught at her hands and forced them back above her head. Gemma was beaten, she knew. She lay completely terrorized, but still attempting to heave him away from her body with violent movements of her hips — the only part of her able to move at all. She writhed against him and her eyes began to blur with a mist of unshed tears as she focused on his face. He was smiling! How could he smile when he was going to kill her? Gemma summoned up all the strength that was left to her and thrust against him. Nothing happened! He had her too secure for escape.

"You'll be giving me entirely the wrong idea if you keep doing that?" he mocked softly. He was hardly out of breath at all, she noted. He was having no trouble though keeping her still.

"You beast . . . " she spat out. "You vulgar swine . . . " Colour flamed in her cheeks and her eyes glittered as she tried to keep the tears of fear and frustration at bay.

"Take it easy," he said calmly. "I was only teasing — trying to inject some humour into the situation."

"Humour!" She almost choked on the word.

"Yes! Humour!" he stated. "God only knows why you took off like that — anybody would think I was Old Nick himself."

"You *are* the devil," she flashed, but lay still now, panting, and knowing she stood no chance of getting away from him.

"Was it because of the gun?"

"Of course it was because of the damn gun," she yelled. "You told me you didn't have one. You lied . . . "

"I *didn't* have one. Not when we first took off from Abbeykirk."

"But you do have one now," she challenged. "You were loading it. What were you intending doing with me? Finishing me off on our afternoon walk? Dumping me in the lake afterwards . . . ?"

A spark of humour lit up the grey eyes above her. "That would have been a terrible waste, wouldn't it?" he said thoughtfully. "I can think of much better uses for you."

"You rat!" she flung at him.

"Who would bake my bread, for instance?" he asked softly.

"Snake!" she hissed.

"Will you promise not to fight me if

166

I free your hands?"

"I'll scratch your damned eyes out," she shrieked and jerked her head sideways in an effort to bring her teeth into contact with one of his hands.

"A nice try," he said sarcastically. "But it won't work, Gemma."

"You're crazy . . . "

"The alternative," he broke in smoothly, "is to stay here like this indefinitely — and I must admit, it's not the most comfortable position in the world."

"Why don't you just shoot me?" she blazed.

"I left the gun behind," he said in all seriousness, and his eyes were lazy, with just a hint of laughter in their depths.

Gemma wriggled her wrists and felt him exert pressure again. "Don't . . . " she squeaked. "You're hurting me . . . "

He held her more carefully then. "You'll probably be a mass of bruises from the tumble," he informed her.

"It's your fault . . . "

"I guess I should have put a bullet through your ankle to stop you, huh?"

Her eyes flew wide at his words and she gasped.

"Just teasing again," he whispered. "The gun isn't real. It's a stage prop." He cocked his head on one side and observed her. "I sneaked it off Tess — she's the star attraction of her local amateur dramatics group."

"I don't believe you." Mutinously Gemma stared up at a lock of blond hair that had fallen forward on his forehead.

"Why are you still alive then?" he asked.

He had a point, she realized. Anyone who had seriously wanted to silence her would have done so, and thoroughly, by now. That was unless he had something more horrifying in store for her before the final reckoning. Inwardly Gemma quaked. "What do you want of me?" she asked, trying to sound brave and keep her voice free from panic.

"Just a promise that you won't 'scratch my damned eyes out'," he challenged.

Gemma clenched her hands into tight fists. He took note of the action. "Point taken," he said reflectively.

Gemma couldn't resist a jibe. "Does your wife know you go in for this sort of thing?" she scorned.

"I don't have a wife." The steely eyes hardened.

"The photograph . . . " she began, but he silenced her swiftly.

"Debra *was* my wife, but not any more."

"I don't blame her for leaving you," Gemma retorted with sadistic pleasure. "You probably gave her just one taste too much of your brutality."

"She wouldn't have left me willingly," he said and it seemed like he was having to hold his emotions rigidly in check. "Debra died," he said then. "She died almost three years ago."

7

"**NO!**" Gemma ceased all movement — even that of her clenched hands. Her words came out jerkily and in a horrified whisper: "Oh, no — Carr — I'm sorry . . . "

"Well, that snippet of information certainly quietened you!" He sighed and his fingers loosened gradually from around her wrists. When she made no move against him, he released her completely. Slowly then, and as if he was still not sure whether to trust her or not, he eased his long weight off her legs. She was free of him then, but still she lay in the green bed of grass with the lake not more than a few yards away. She didn't move, not even when he crouched beside her and smiled down into her face. Some of the tenseness had left him now. "You're free," he reminded her gently.

Gemma eased up onto one elbow, wincing a little as she became aware of a soreness in her shoulder where she'd crashed to the ground. "Carr?" Her eyes were deep pools of incomprehension. She wanted to know what had happened to Debra.

"You want to know about Debra?" The name came easily to his lips. She nodded and pushed herself to a sitting position, wriggling her shoulder painfully? "Does it hurt?" he asked — as if he really cared.

"I fell on it."

"Let me see." Carefully he slipped her jacket off, then gently he checked her arm and shoulder for ease of movement. "Nothing broken," he said at last. "But I'm sorry I had to be so rough with you."

She stared at him. The shoulder didn't matter at all and she wanted to tell him so. Somehow, even the fact that he might be the gunman didn't have the power to frighten her quite so much either. For the very first time she had learnt something important about him. Carr Winterton had once had a wife — but that wife had died.

"Are you really interested in Debra?" he asked.

"Only if you feel you can tell me."

"She was killed in a road accident." There was pain in his eyes, though he wasn't asking for sympathy, she knew. His lips twisted into a little grimace that was almost a smile. "Deb was five months pregnant at the time, so I lost both of them."

"Oh, Carr . . . " She reached out her hand. It touched his arm lightly and he glanced down at it. He made no attempt to restrain her now, knowing there was no need. The fight had gone out of her.

"I'm still the same man," he said quietly. "Your knowing about Debra hasn't changed me."

"I know!" Resigned, she stared at him. "It seems to make you more human though."

"Having a wife? Lots of criminals have wives and families, Gemma."

"You keep telling me you're *not* a criminal," she pointed out.

"Let's get you up out of that damp grass," he said in a practical voice. "I never intended you getting close enough to me to pierce my armour, lady — but it seems you have." He reached out and helped her to her feet.

That done, he bent down and picked up her jacket. On the way back to the house he slipped it round her shoulders, and once at the door, he urged her back inside and towards the kitchen — the warmest room in the place. Gemma shivered in a chair beside the stove while he made a pot of steaming tea from the kettle that always seemed to be on the boil. When it was ready he brought her a mug and placed it between her numbed fingers. "Drink up," he said cheerfully. "It'll warm you."

"Thanks!" Gratefully she sipped at the tea.

Carr leaned against the table with his own drink. "Feel like telling me what brought on the panic?" he asked.

"I — I told you. The gun!" Gemma warmed her hands around the glazed pot and didn't dare look directly at him.

"You really do think I'm that guy who held you up, don't you?" he said steadily.

Fear crept into her eyes again. "You could be," she hedged.

"And as I told you before, the description you gave of him could fit any one of a thousand others," he said.

"Do you think I don't realize that too?" For a moment fire flashed in her eyes. "Do you think I haven't tried to convince myself that you're *not* him, these past two days?"

"I don't suppose it's any good me telling you — emphatically — that I'm not a bank robber or a killer?"

"No good at all," she replied flatly.

"Then we'd better get on with our

lives just the way they are," he suggested and with the words pushed himself away from the table. He took his mug over to the sink.

"Just like that!" Gemma retorted, warmed through now and feeling much more in control.

"Just like that, my sweet." The reply was vehement. He turned back to her just as she rose from her seat. He took a step towards her — held out his hand. Uncertainly she backed away. "For goodness sake," he ground out. "It's only the cup I want."

Gemma banged the mug down on the table and marched purposefully towards the door.

"Where do you think you're going?" he asked.

She swung round impatiently. "Out!"

"No you're not." The intense gaze was raking her, warning her.

"I need some air," she protested.

"Forget it, Gemma."

Danger signals prickled all the length of her spine at the chill in his tone.

"You can't seriously expect me to stay incarcerated in here all the time," she flung at him.

"I offered to take you walking," he reminded her. "But you chose to run out on me."

"Only because of the gun . . . "

"I'm not prepared to risk a repeat performance," he said, and an exacting little smiled tugged at the corners of his mouth.

She faced him. "Are you telling me I'm a prisoner?" Her chin tilted defiantly.

He gave nothing away either by his expression or his voice. "For the time being — yes." He swept her mug up from the table, then returned to the sink.

* * *

Gemma waited to hear no more. Her pride, however, would not allow her to run this time. She was halfway to the front door when she realized she'd left her jacket in the kitchen. It was cold outside, she remembered; she'd need the coat for there had been a ground frost that morning. But she couldn't go back, she reasoned. It would make too much of a mockery of her grand exit if she did. Her hand was already on the night-latch when he stopped her. It was almost as if he'd decided to see how far she'd go, because he could have caught her before she'd left the kitchen if he'd wanted. One lean, hard hand descended on hers. She could feel his body close up behind her. "Don't make me do this," he warned, and there was deliberation in the cool voice.

Gemma's breath caught in her throat. "You . . . you can't keep me here," she said, but even to her own ears her words held little conviction.

"Gemma! Be reasonable!" She heard his breath hiss out in a sigh of resignation.

A frosty dignity made her hold herself erect. "Take your hands off me." Her fingers curled round the latch. It was becoming a battle of wills now.

His movement was swift. He twisted her hand away from the door-latch and with the same easy action spun her round to face him. "God, you make life difficult." His tone was clipped and there was a ruthless purpose etched on his features.

★ ★ ★

Some frail thread of reason warned her not to provoke him. She bit back the bitter words of scorn that had sprung to her lips. Her eyes came into contact with his and they were so close now, their bodies were touching. His free hand came up to rest on the door panel at the side of her head, and then his head curved down and her own tilted back so that her chin pointed delicately towards him. He still gripped her wrist, but suddenly Gemma found herself twisting her fingers, curling them round his and holding him tightly. Her lips were eager for the touch of him — the taste of him. She didn't want to fight him any more. She closed her eyes and felt hard little kisses mouthed against her lips, then down to her throat. In seconds he had claimed her mouth again, this time more masterfully than before. Gemma drew in her breath at the sweetness, the fulfilment of the kiss that followed. Her lips parted softly and Carr Winterton took full advantage of the fact. Some wild reason warned her that she oughtn't to be enjoying this at all. Her mind made a feeble attempt to resist the urgent pressure of his lips, but logic and reason were lost in the wild surge of ecstasy that had her pressing her body against him and feeling the response of his arousal.

He raised his head slowly and Gemma's eyes flew open to lock with his in silent understanding. There was a rough kind of gentleness in his voice as he admitted softly, "Well, that was supposed to teach you a lesson, but I guess it did the same for me."

"Carr . . . " Her voice was husky and weak.

"I think maybe we should occupy ourselves with some safer pastime," he said thoughtfully, and his hand unclasped from hers and he let it fall to his side.

"The . . . the books . . . " she whispered hesitantly, holding herself rigidly in check so that she wouldn't throw herself into his arms.

"Yes! Do you mind being there with me — in the 'spider's parlour' with all the dust?"

She shook her head and cleared her mind — or tried to — of the events of the past few minutes. "No . . . " She was so breathless she couldn't say more. No doubt he was thinking she'd been an easy push-over, she told herself.

★ ★ ★

For the rest of the afternoon it was difficult trying to pretend that nothing had happened between them. He tried — she knew he tried — to put her at ease by being particularly nice. But Gemma was watchful of his every move. After the evening meal it was no better. They began a game of cards but there was an atmosphere of tension and of feelings being held rigidly in check, even though there was a table breadth between them. Every time their eyes met or their fingers touched accidentally, Gemma would spring away. In desperation she pushed the cards away. "I can't keep my mind on this," she muttered irritably.

Carr glanced at the watch on his wrist. "It's nine-thirty," he said. "Perhaps an early night will do us both good."

"Do you mind if I take a book up . . . ?" Her words were stilted and unnatural.

"You'll ruin your eyesight," he warned with a smile. "There's only the oil-lamp up there."

"That's all we have down here."

Gemma gazed up at the one suspended on chains from the ceiling.

He grinned, and muttered, "I suppose so. I think I'll take one up, too."

"*You* don't have to stay awake," she protested. "I'd hardly try to run out on you in the middle of the night, would I?"

"You might," he said as he cleared the playing-cards with a single sweep of one hand. "You're headstrong enough to try it."

* * *

It was more in the nature of feeling around in the semi-darkness than actually choosing a book. Carr had placed the oil-lamp from the parlour on a table at the bottom of the stairs earlier, so only the borrowed light managed to penetrate the gloominess. She pulled the first book her hand alighted on from the packing-case. She could see it had a hard, glossy jacket. Gemma peered closely at it. Some of the books they had unpacked earlier had been either classics or popular fiction. This particular one had a picture of an oil-rig on its front. She hadn't taken much note of titles earlier. All day long her mind had been on other things.

Gemma clutched the book tightly under her arm. Carr was waiting at the foot of the stairs. He gave a little smile. "Action-adventure," he said, nodding briefly at the book. "Not the best sleep-inducer."

Gemma didn't feel much like exchanging pleasantries. "It was the first one I picked up." She scowled. "How *anyone* manages to live without electricity I'll never know," she rebuked sourly.

"I promise to have it installed by the time you come here again," he placated.

Gemma swept past him and marched up the stairs. Any effect of cool disdain, however, was lost at the top of the stairs, for here the drab, worn carpet ended and her sensible building society shoes clattered in an altogether uncomplimentary fashion on the bare floorboards. She'd worn them for the trip outside and had never got round to changing them, she realized.

She called, "Goodnight!" as she swept into her bedroom, then stopped as she realized the place was in darkness. "Damn!" She'd forgotten all about not having a light. She fumbled around to see if he'd left matches there the night before, for then he'd gone up early and lit lamps in both bedrooms. A shadow darkened her doorway even more and, alarmed, she whirled.

"It's only me," he said softly. "You'll need a lamp. For heaven's sake stop panicking, girl."

"I — I'm not!" She cowered into herself as he came fully into the room, then held her body rigid so that she wouldn't accidentally brush against him.

"Yes, you are," he said easily and promptly moved over to light the lamp for her. In the subdued radiance of the glow as he replaced the shade, his hair was like pale wheat with the sun on it. The light threw his features into relief and he seemed stern — though not frighteningly so. He straightened when he'd adjusted the flame. "Sleep tight," he murmured as he passed her so close that she could feel the casual touch of his arm and inhaled the scent of his skin too. It was pleasantly musk with expensive aftershave, but homely too with the dusty bouquet of old books still upon him.

"Goodnight, Carr . . . " Until that moment, Gemma had never realized just how much she'd missed having a man's body close beside her at nights. She tried to remember a time when she and Keith had been close — but not just physically close. That time seemed far away now, and surprisingly she felt no bitterness towards Keith any more. Carr Winterton wouldn't treat her as a mother-figure, she felt sure . . . God! What was she thinking of? The events of the afternoon must have turned her head. She dare not dwell on the memory of Carr's kisses.

* * *

Gemma closed the door firmly upon him, then leaned back against it breathing hard. She never heard his own bedroom door latch. Maybe he'd be sleeping with it open just so she wouldn't get past him and down the stairs, she mused. On the other hand, he could just be checking that gun again — the one he'd told her was a stage prop. Not that she'd believed such a story! Did he really think he'd taken her in with it? She was glad it hadn't made a reappearance however, and he hadn't even mentioned it again. Carr Winterton was an altogether too complex man, she decided. He was a complete mystery to her — and a liar into the bargain, she had to remind herself. She sat down with a thud on the end of her narrow little bed. Idly she picked up the book she'd brought upstairs. " . . . a novel by Carr Winter . . . " she read. She flipped it open and inside, the dedication read: 'For Debra'!

★ ★ ★

So — it hadn't *all* been lies. He really was a writer. Did that mean perhaps that he hadn't lied also about the gun?

8

GEMMA'S sleep was troubled that night. She didn't close her eyes until well into the early hours and then it was only after determining to question Carr Winterton about his writing. It did seem likely, however, that he was in fact the author of the book she had taken up to bed. It was too much of a coincidence for him not to be, her mind reasoned. But it did *not* explain his interest in her — or why he had taken it upon himself to bring her here to this house called Black Gill Croft. Her head objected in the most violent manner when bright sunlight from the window squeezed through her lashes the following morning. Gemma groaned and turned her face to the wall. Someone knocked at the door. It sounded like an army thundering to get in. "Go away," she wailed, and the pillow vibrated agonizingly to the sound of her voice. He rapped on the door again.

"Gemma! Are you all right?" Did she detect a note of concern?

"Go away!" The whimper took her all her time to get it out and she hung onto her head with both hands to prevent any movement. She couldn't face him like this — she just couldn't.

"Gemma!" This time he demanded attention. She pushed herself down under the warm brushed cotton sheets and disregarded the alarm-bells that told her to expect trouble if she didn't let him in. It never occurred to her until it was too late, to remember that the door had no lock or key. The next time he spoke her name it was nearer somehow. "Gemma!" The springy mattress gave slightly on its edge and Gemma tensed, only then recalling the lack of a key to her room. She felt his hand on the blanket just above her shoulder. "Gemma — for God's sake . . . "

"Just let me die in peace," she muttered irritably.

She heard the relief in his voice. "Headache?" he asked patiently, and with the word, pulled her carefully over onto her back.

Gemma screwed up her eyes against the sun that was invading the room with more insistence now. Without speaking again, Carr got up from the bed and walked over to the tiny window. Quietly he pulled the curtains across so that the room was plunged into dark shadow.

"Is that better?" He came back to her and with concern so as not to jar her, sat on the edge of the bed once more.

"No!" She hated him being so close and she so helpless.

"Your eyes are open anyway," he comforted. "Care to ease up on those pillows now?"

"No!" She flung her head aside and winced as sharp arrows criss-crossed her head.

"I've brought you a cup of tea."

"The cure for all ills," she replied

acidly, keeping her gaze fixed firmly on the wall.

"You're feeling much better already — I can tell," he said with heavy sarcasm.

"I need sugar when I'm feeling like this," she protested.

"I guessed you would," he said, bending down and retrieving the cup and saucer from the floor. "You didn't sleep for a good three-quarters of the night, did you?"

"So — I kept you awake, too, did I?" Gemma asked, feeling smug because of that knowledge at least, and allowing herself to face him again.

"I'm a very light sleeper." He bestowed a grin on her. "Come on now, sit up and drink this."

"You're eager." She pushed herself up awkwardly, then eyed the tea. "Is it poisoned?"

"Taste it and see," came the swift reply as he handed her the drink.

"Arsenic?" she asked sweetly when she'd taken a sip.

"Belladonna," he stated seriously. "I grow it out in the back garden in that tangle of weeds. It doesn't have such a giveaway taste as arsenic — especially when sugar is added."

The tea revived her. She pulled a face at him. "I hate men who make jokes first thing in the mornings." Drums still pounded in her head but they were more muffled now. She finished the drink, then politely held out the cup and saucer to him. She lowered her gaze to rest it on the cool, white bedspread. "I'm sorry," she muttered. "I ought to at least thank you . . ."

"Will breakfast in twenty minutes suit you?"

Gemma's face was pale. She slid down on the pillows. "I'll get down," she promised. "Somehow!"

"You really have got a head, haven't you?" Suddenly he cared.

"I stayed up late reading the book. Then I couldn't sleep."

"I didn't realize it was that bad."

"My head?" she asked, puzzled.

"The book!" He grinned again.

"It wasn't. I enjoyed it. Did you write it, Carr?"

"The first one I ever did," he revealed.

"It was good."

"Flatterer!" He pushed the hair back from her forehead in a casual little gesture. "My later ones are a lot more believable," he said drily.

"Have you been on an oil-rig?" she wanted to know. "Because it was believable."

"Never in my life — I'd be scared of falling off," he teased.

"I don't think you'd ever be scared of anything," she said solemnly.

"I'm not the stuff heroes are made of," he said. "I just write about those kind of guys."

"Well, I liked it."

"Thank you!" He stood up and looked down on her. "I'll have to find you one of my murder-mystery ones."

"Do you write from experience, Mr Winterton?" Gemma asked mockingly.

"You really are determined not to trust me, aren't you," he replied, but there was a smile in his voice.

Realizing that she was hardly in a position to start another argument, Gemma kept silent. Lying in a stranger's bed and clad only in a brief cotton nightshirt wasn't really the time to antagonize him, she knew. "You said something about breakfast . . . " she reminded him lightly.

He moved over to the door. "Twenty minutes," he said, and then he was gone.

★ ★ ★

Gemma walked across the kitchen and hesitated beside the table. She wanted to make up for being so out of sorts earlier, but didn't really know how to go about it. She pushed her hands deep into the pockets of her trousers and glowered at his back view as he stood beside the stove.

"Would you like to pour the tea?" His voice startled her. She hadn't realized he knew she was there.

"Yes! Yes . . . of course!" Flustered, she picked up the teapot.

"How's the head?" He spared her a brief glance.

"Better — much better — thanks," she muttered.

"There's aspirin in the cupboard." He nodded at the one against the window. "Paracetamol, too."

"It's okay — really."

He brought plates over to the table, looking casually assured of himself and dressed in a light-grey sweatshirt. A faint smile touched his lips but not his eyes. Gemma's heart churned inside her and in trying to appear nonchalant herself, the teapot slipped from her fingers and crashed onto the table, spilling its contents on the wooden surface. "Don't worry about it." He reached for a cloth and mopped up the splashes.

Gemma tried to apologize calmly but failed. "I'm s-sorry . . . "

"I said not to worry!" He glanced across the table at her. "There's no harm been done, sit down now and eat up."

Her chair scraped across the tiled floor as she eased herself into it. She couldn't look at him, though under lowered lashes she was aware of him sitting down opposite. Breakfast didn't take long, at least not for Gemma. It was difficult forcing scrambled eggs past the lump that for some reason had formed in her throat. She wished she had been more pleasant to him that morning, but her head had ached so badly . . . She drank down her cup of tea, then pushed her plate away.

"Aren't you hungry?"

"I — I've eaten most of it." Gemma eyed her plate which was far from empty. Awkwardly she rose to her feet and began to collect the cups and saucers.

As he'd done before, he helped her

wash up the things, and she wished that he wouldn't but dare not say so. She was becoming familiar with the layout of the numerous cupboards and drawers and within ten minutes she had the whole lot sparkling and spotless, having wiped down every surface possible.

Carr didn't speak much. When everything was finished he leaned silently against a worktop and watched her busying herself. "It's fine, Gemma," he said. "Just leave it now, will you?"

"Would you like me to prepare lunch today?" she asked.

"It's my turn, I think," he replied patiently. "And there's still plenty of bread left over for a couple of days."

She lifted her shoulders in a helpless little gesture, then wrapped her arms around herself as she gazed out through the tiny window. "So — what do we do now?"

"We sit tight."

"Can't we go outside," Gemma pleaded.

"And risk a repeat performance of

yesterday's little fiasco?" His brows drew together in a frown and Gemma felt her cheeks beginning to warm uncomfortably.

"Are you going to hold that against me for all time?" she asked in a huff.

"Why not? You seem to regard me as public enemy number one," he shot back.

Irritated more than she dared let him know, Gemma turned her back on him completely. "If you're going to take that attitude I may as well go back up to my bedroom," she snapped.

"Suit yourself, Gemma." She heard him move away and knew her path to the door was clear.

There was nothing for it then but to walk as unconcernedly as she knew how, past him and to the open door. Once she'd passed through it, however, she was somewhat taken aback to realize that he really was going to let her go back to her room. For some reason she'd been certain he would try and stop her. Guiltily, she had to admit to herself that she'd almost hoped he would. Sitting upstairs alone, in a cold little bedroom, did not appeal. She wondered idly what his reaction would be if she were to walk calmly out of the front door instead of turning away to the stairs. Perhaps he wouldn't even notice, she mused, especially if she closed the kitchen door between them first. It might be worth a try . . .

"Leave the door open, Gemma." The clear, clipped voice must have read her thoughts.

Her head was still aching and for some reason she felt like bursting into tears. Carr Winterton didn't usually speak to her in so abrupt a manner. Perhaps if she were to apologize . . . make the headache an excuse for her irritability . . . No! She drew herself up and forced ice into her voice. "Perhaps you should learn a little about trust yourself before expecting it of me, Carr." She swung away then towards the stairs.

Tears stung her eyes as she clattered along the corridor to her bedroom. He didn't follow and she never heard if he'd made any reply to her outburst. For most of the morning she heard him moving about downstairs, mainly in the kitchen area of the house. She tried to read more of the book she'd borrowed the previous night, but her mind refused to take in any of the printed words. When she became cold she pulled a blanket round her shoulders and stood looking out over the lake. Its surface was flat and grey, with reflections of skeletal trees on it. The gently sloping hillside on the opposite shore was dark with autumn tints: amber, scarlet, russet. Leaves lay thickly on the ground. On a sunny day the colours would be spectacular. Even in today's dull mistiness the scene had a subdued beauty. Her eye caught a movement on the hill between the trees. It was gone in a flash, but had definitely been there.

It could have been something — or someone — drifting out from behind a tree-trunk and then darting back again. An angle of light had caught something metallic — a camera? Or spectacles? It might just as easily have been binoculars — or . . . a gun? Gemma stared out across the water until her eyes were sore from straining. All was quiet downstairs. Uneasily she wondered if Carr, too, had seen the movement. She tried not to think about it, because right then in a tiny corner of her mind was the suspicion that *he* might have been expecting a signal or something. About to turn back into the room, she saw it again — and this time there was no doubt at all. It was a man — a heavily coated figure — standing against one of the trees and successfully blending into the background. He was too far away for her to make out his features or colouring — but there was no doubt about what he was doing. *He was watching the house!*

9

GEMMA froze against the curtain, shivering now — not from the cold, but from fear. The house oozed silence and that unnerved her. That menacing figure on the far bank of the lake never moved. At times she could almost convince herself that it wasn't human at all but a smaller tree perhaps, or a trick of the light. She glanced at her watch and saw it was twelve-fifteen. Carr still hadn't called her down for lunch. She wondered uneasily if he were teaching her a lesson and making her go without food. Her eyes strayed back to the interior of the room then back again to the hillside across the lake. The figure had gone! She began to wish she hadn't condemned herself to solitary confinement. At half past the hour, Gemma decided to go in search of Carr and to hell with her pride. The stairs creaked at number two, five and seven despite the rough carpeting. As she approached the hall, by leaning slightly over the balustrade she could see that the kitchen door was still open. Of Carr, however, there was no sign. Anger became uppermost in her mind then, for she began to convince herself he had gone out and left her alone. But as she reached the kitchen door she caught a glimpse of him standing quiet and still against the window. He was looking out over the lake, just as she had been doing herself in the bedroom above the kitchen. He seemed absorbed in something and didn't at first hear her. It wasn't until she pushed the door wider that he turned abruptly to face her. Did she imagine his unease? But almost immediately his preoccupation with the scene outside the window was replaced with an easy, light-hearted banter. "Did you enjoy your read?"

A bitter reply sprang to her lips. With difficulty she forced it down and even managed an insipid little smile. "Yes, thanks!"

"Did you finish the book?"

"No! It was too cold up there to sit any longer. I had to take a blanket off the bed and wrap it round me."

His smile told her he had known it would be cold. "You could have come back down here," he said.

"I didn't think I'd be welcome!"

"I'm not going to argue, Gemma." He turned away to the stove and pulled open the oven door. He'd cooked huge potatoes in their jackets, she saw, and on the table was cheese and floury hunks of bread.

"I thought you'd gone out. It was so quiet." She sat down at the table and he brought coffee over in a jug and poured it into two mugs.

"You think I'd do that? And leave you alone here?"

Gemma lifted her shoulders then sipped at her coffee. Both her hands were wrapped around the mug for warmth. Carr sat down facing her and handed her the plate of bread. "Thanks!" She stared down at her plate.

"What have you been doing up there if not reading?" he wanted to know.

"Watching the birds on the lake . . . " Abruptly she stopped, aware of his dark gaze resting on her face. "I . . . I told you . . . I wrapped myself in a blanket . . . " It was difficult trying to hoodwink him!

"Did you see anything else?" he asked lightly.

Gemma concentrated hard on the potato on her plate and made sure her voice was steady as she replied, "Should I have done?" This time it was her turn to be direct. She levelled a solemn stare at Carr Winterton.

"Sometimes young deer come down to the water's edge," he replied, as if he'd had the statement all ready and waiting.

"I'll have to watch more closely, won't I?" She smiled at him, but had the uneasy feeling that he could see right through her and wasn't in the least taken in by her words. He didn't bring up the subject again though, and Gemma began to think she was letting her imagination run away with her.

As they cleared away after the meal, she made herself ask pleasantly, "Any chance of a walk outside this afternoon, Carr?"

"None at all," he said and the question was there in his eyes again.

* * *

That day passed somehow and the next was no better. She couldn't bring herself to trust him completely and yet the attraction between them grew stronger with every hour they spent together. By the afternoon of the fifth day, Gemma was too restless to give her mind to anything at all. The little house was spotless and shining. She'd cleaned and polished it from top to bottom. All Carr's books were now crowded neatly onto the shelves in sitting-room and study. Carr himself had almost stripped the staircase of its age-old varnish too. It seemed as if they both made a conscious effort to work hard and keep out of each other's way as much as possible. Gemma had begged him to allow her to go outside for some fresh air, but he repeatedly refused her pleas. She decided to try him one more time. There had been no sign of anyone on the hillside opposite again and Gemma could almost imagine now that the figure had been some trick of the light and not real at all.

"Carr — I need some sort of activity," she grumbled. "*Why* can't I just go out there and jog on the spot for ten minutes?"

"Don't you call it activity — what you've been doing in here?" he asked.

"Housework!" Gemma managed to make the word sound like an obscenity. "Don't patronize me, please, Carr." She faced him squarely, hands thrust into the pockets of her blue jeans.

They were in the spotless kitchen and Carr turned away to the kettle to make yet another cup of coffee. She felt like screaming. "Not *more* coffee!" She grimaced. "It must be all this sitting around drinking coffee that's making me jumpy. I'll soon have caffeine poisoning!"

"It's decaffeinated," he said pleasantly. "Find another excuse, Gemma my sweet."

"Boredom?" she asked innocently, tilting her head to one side and gazing up at him.

Carr replaced the kettle and walked round the table to her. He placed his hands lightly on her shoulders. "Cat-green eyes you may have," he said, "and now you've got the same expression on your face as my mother's pet Siamese kitten when it wants some cream — but it won't work with me, Gemma. You can turn on all the charm you like, but you're still not going outside — not even if you begin to purr."

"Why not?" Her gaze was stormy.

"You know why not. You don't really have to ask."

"I don't know what you mean . . . "

Calmly the grey eyes watched her. "You saw the man, didn't you?" he said at last, not loosening his grip on her at all.

"M — man?" She swallowed nervously and transferred her gaze to the table-top.

"On the hillside opposite," he stated.

"How do you know that?" Her eyes swept up to him then. "I never said . . . "

"You didn't have to say anything — it was written all over your face when you came downstairs," he said.

He was taking it all very calmly, Gemma thought. "So — what if I did?" She tossed her head and never wavered.

"He wasn't any buddy of mine, Gemma."

She drew in her breath sharply. "Do you think . . . "

209

"It's logical to believe it could be," he said.

"Then why hasn't he done something? Why doesn't he try to get at me?" Gemma's lips were dry; she felt tense all over.

"He hasn't had a good look at you. He can't be sure it's you, can he? Added to that, these walls are over a foot thick — he'd need a cannon to shoot from over there."

"Do you think he's still there?"

He hesitated only slightly before replying. "It's more than possible."

"Oh, God!" Her voice was a squeak. Gemma resolved not to panic. "I am not going to panic," she said forcefully. "But just get me out of this, will you, Carr?"

He nodded and agreed tersely. "Yes. I'd already decided to do that — tonight."

"Why not right now?" she demanded.

"Sitting ducks, remember?" His lips twisted into a grim little smile.

"But we won't be able to see him if

we wait until dark . . . "

"That works both ways, Gemma. He won't see us either."

Wide-eyed, she stared at him. "What you mean is that he won't be able to see *me*!"

"*Us!*" he corrected. "We're in this together. My plan is to slip out later and bring the car right up to the door if possible."

"He won't let you . . . " Dismay suddenly took hold of her and she trembled at the thought of being left alone in the house. "And you can't get much nearer the house," she reminded him. "There are boulders and long grass and bushes . . . "

"So I'll come as near as I can," he said. "Don't worry, Gemma, John Franklyn knows you're here. If he thinks there's any real danger he'll be doing something about it."

"How can he know."

"I phoned your boss, remember?"

She only had his word for that, Gemma recalled, but now was not the time to start up her doubting all over again. "I'm scared," she whispered. "We're a long way from anywhere out here. Anything could happen."

"But nothing has," he said quietly and his hands were firm on her shoulders. "And that means he's not sure it's you I've got here."

"He — he's waiting to get a good look at me . . . "

"He must be. He's waited five days already."

"You do have that gun though . . . "

"Gemma!" He sighed heavily. "I've told you — it isn't a real gun. It's a stage prop, and although it makes a loud noise it won't do any lasting damage. It might just scare our friend out there, but it isn't dangerous. One shot directly at him and he'd know we were bluffing."

Gemma looked doubtful, still not fully believing the easy explanation about the gun. "I saw you loading a cartridge," she accused.

"You load blanks just like the real

thing," he explained, and instantly let go of her shoulders and moved away to the table.

"You don't have to keep up the pretence, you know," she challenged.

"Gemma!" He swung round to face her, his patience stretched to the limit. "Gemma, believe me, I am *not* a liar — and I'm not a damned bank robber either, or a would-be killer. I'm a writer. You've seen some of my books; you've read one yourself. Carr Winter — that's me. What more can I say to convince you?"

"Being a writer doesn't make you a damn saint," she cried. "I suppose there have been writers who were on the wrong side of the law."

"I give up," he sighed, striding away to the kettle again. She watched as he poured hot water into the two mugs, then he brought them to the table and pushed one across at her. "Just trust me, Gemma," he said. "You don't really have much choice, do you? There's nobody else riding up on a white charger just at the moment to help you."

"If you were in my place . . . "

"I'd probably be scared as hell too," he broke in. "But don't forget, he's got to get past me to get at you."

"It isn't *your* problem. You didn't see him. You didn't go on television and say you *saw* him."

"So — if it isn't *my* problem, do I just turf you out of here and let you fend for yourself?" he asked bitingly.

Gemma caught her bottom lip between her teeth, then replied quietly, "I'd rather you didn't."

"So trust me," he said and pulled up a chair and sat down.

"Why the hell don't you have an in-car telephone?" she asked with resignation.

"I've never seen the necessity for one — until now."

Gemma scowled over the rim of her cup, knowing she was being unreasonable. "So what are we going to do?"

"I've told you," he said patiently. "As soon as it's dusk, I'll go out the back way — skirt the cottage, keeping under cover of the stone wall out there, and make my way to the car."

"Then I make a run for it . . . "

"No! Then I'll come and get you. I'll leave the engine running and make a dash to the front door where you will be waiting."

"Why can't *I* just make the dash while you wait in the car — we could get away more quickly then."

"Be reasonable, Gemma," he pleaded. "Two moving targets are better than one. If he is out there, he won't know which one of us to fire at first."

"I don't like it, Carr . . . "

"Neither do I, my sweet, but it's the best I can come up with."

"And you *will* have the gun . . . ?"

"Which won't hurt anybody," he said sceptically. "You still don't believe me about that, though, do you?"

"Why don't you prove to me that it's harmless?" she asked quietly. "Why don't you just bring it down here and let fly at something so I'll know?"

"It would arouse suspicion if that guy's out there."

"You're *very* convincing, Mister Winterton," she jibed.

He clasped his hands on the table in front of him. "Look, Gemma," he said, "maybe I can *write* crime — but I can't do the real thing. I don't believe in violence. I doubt if I could pull the trigger if somebody was standing in front of me with the most lethal weapon ever invented. This is the first time in my life I've come up against real danger — and it's not to my liking. I'm ordinary — I'm not the stuff heroes are made of."

Gemma could have disputed the statement about him being ordinary. Carr Winterton was fast approaching the hero mark in her estimation. Even though at times she distrusted him, she couldn't help but like him. "You're remarkably cool-headed," she responded quickly.

"Possibly because I've done it all before — but *only* on paper," he pointed out. "I have a logical mind — I have to figure things out for my story lines. I do a lot of research in order to get the facts right. I've even talked to criminals to find out how their minds work."

"So — how much research does it need to write a bank robbery?" Gemma couldn't help asking, but she was totally unprepared for his reaction. He pushed his coffee-mug away and rose to his feet, almost upsetting his chair as he did so. Then he strode round the table and jerked her roughly up from her seat. Almost lifted off her feet, Gemma felt a tingle of pure shock go right through her. His mouth was set in severe lines.

"Right!" he said. "You've asked for it, madam!" He was breathing hard in an effort to keep himself in check. "I'll show you the damn gun. Come with me." He gave her no choice but to accompany him as he gripped her arm fiercely and half led, half dragged her out into the hall.

"Carr . . . no . . . " she wailed.

"Gemma! Yes!" He began to haul her up the stairs.

She stumbled and hung onto the balustrade. "I — I didn't mean . . . " she began.

Exasperated, he stopped and faced her. "Yes, you did," he said and his anger was all but evaporated now. A hopeless expression clouded his eyes. "You've intimated just once too often that I'm the bastard who robbed your precious building society, Gemma."

"No . . . please . . . " Fear filled her voice and fluttered through her stomach. He was strong — he was confident and his fingers curved around her hand that was clenched firmly on the wooden rail. Gently but easily he prised her away from her anchor. Gemma found herself being pulled up the stairs then. Her breath was coming out in deep sobs by the time they reached the top. Her mind shied away from the fact that he kicked open his bedroom door and she tried not to scream as he propelled her inside and then slammed it shut again behind them. Wildly her eyes sought for some form of defence. They alighted on the gun, resting on top of the bedside cabinet. He leaned back against the door and released her hand and Gemma wasted no time. She covered the space between herself and the bed in record time to whip up the gun and, her hand shaking visibly, point it directly at Carr Winterton.

* * *

To her horror, he began to laugh. It was a softly controlled sound but all the more menacing for that. Up until then, though he'd been furious with her, he'd tried not to let it show. The man who had held her up had been calm and ruthless. Gemma's thin thread of patience snapped. The gun was heavy — surely it wouldn't weigh so much if it were in fact just a toy. She took aim, not actually at his head but at a point several feet higher. She didn't feel at all brave, but she *was* seethingly angry — and scared too. He wasn't laughing now, she noted. He was looking at her in a most disquieting manner. It made her want to throw the gun down and run to him to beg his forgiveness for what she had contemplated doing.

"Don't fire it, Gemma!"

"But it's harmless," she said. "You told me so yourself."

"It will arouse suspicion if anyone is outside."

"It might also kill you," she retorted.

He shook his head slowly and smiled, then he held out one hand. "Give it to me, Gemma."

"No! Stay where you are." Her arm was beginning to ache with the pull on her wrist muscle.

"I can't let you do it." He took a step forward.

"Stay there," she shrieked.

"Gemma — be reasonable."

"I'll fire it. I *will*, Carr . . . "

"Do you know how to?" he asked, and there was a hint of humour in his voice again.

"It — it's easy . . . "

"Have you ever done it before? Killed somebody?" he wanted to know.

"Carr — I'm warning you."

"You've never even held a gun, have you?" he said easily.

Gemma thrust her chin up obstinately. "I do know what to do."

"You'll make a good job of it at this range," he said lightly. "You do realize, don't you, that your aim will drop slightly with the force of the shot?"

"Shut up," she yelled.

"Do you think you'll be able to drag me away from the door when you've blown my head off?" he asked in the most casual of manners.

"Damn you . . . " Gemma's stomach revolted at the thought of what he'd said.

"Nervous?" He took another step towards her, smiling as he did so.

She backed away and felt the springy mattress of his bed right behind her knees. "No!" she snapped in what she hoped was a convincing tone.

"You don't really want to do it, do you?"

"No," she agreed, "I don't — but if I have to, I will."

"I'm going to take the gun off you, sweetheart." He began to walk purposefully across the room.

"Don't even try . . . " Gemma's face paled.

He came nearer, not even hesitating now, and Gemma steadied the gun with both hands. At the last moment she jerked it to point upwards at the ceiling — and fired!

★ ★ ★

She wasn't prepared for the explosion that ripped at her eardrums — and she hadn't expected the empty cartridge to catapult out of the back of the gun as it did. She screamed and reeled away and to one side, seeing Carr reaching out to her, his face furious. She never intended pulling the trigger a second time; it must have been a purely reflex action to do so. But, dismayed, she saw him clutch at his stomach as the second echo died away, and then he collapsed groaning onto the bed.

"No! No!" Terror raced through her and her heart battered wildly in her chest. There was a pungent, biting smell lingering in the air. A sob caught in her throat and she hurled the weapon away into the farthest corner of the room. The man on the bed was silent. He was lying face-down across the beige and black geometrically figured quilt. Gemma sprang to life as she realized what she had done. Tears began to cascade helplessly down her cheeks. "Carr . . . Carr . . . " She was beside him in seconds, kneeling there on the bed and tugging at his shoulders with hands that were trembling and inadequate. He was still warm, she reasoned, as somehow she managed to haul the dead weight of him over onto his back. She stared down at the man, seeing the blond, dishevelled head, the closed eyes that no longer mocked her. She placed her hand against his throat, feeling for a pulse above the silvery striped collar of his shirt. Thankfully he was still alive — but for how long, she wondered? Panic began to make itself known. Tears poured down her cheeks. He'd done her no harm, she knew. He'd been good to her. Now he was lying helpless, perhaps dying, and it was all her fault. Then there was this dreadful feeling she had that part of her was dying, too. She couldn't — wouldn't — put a name to it. All she did know in that moment was that if she'd really killed him, then she didn't care what happened to her either. Nothing mattered at all, except the inert man before her. But there seemed nothing she could do now to save him.

10

GEMMA ran her hands over his shoulders and body. There was no blood in evidence. She tried to recall just where she'd been aiming the gun when it had gone off. Her mind drew a blank. Everything had happened so quickly. All the time, tears scalded her cheeks as she sobbed out his name. In desperation she bent down low over him and laid her ear against his chest, feeling with nervous fingers for the steady beat of his heart, but half afraid she wouldn't find it.

"You're making my shirt all wet," a lazy voice informed her softly. "But it feels nice having you there all the same."

Gemma's head jerked up and her eyes, red-rimmed and thoroughly shocked, focused on his face.

Laughter was not far away from the

teasing grey eyes, but even as she made an effort to spring away from him, one steel-banded arm hooked round her waist, overbalancing her from her kneeling position on the bed, and toppling her against his body.

"Carr . . . you're hurt . . . " Her voice was a mere whimper of sound.

"Blanks don't hurt anyone, sweetheart," he mocked, and his lips were dangerously close to hers. His free hand came up to ruffle the dark, dishevelled curls, then gently he smoothed his fingers across her cheek, wiping away the tears. "I'm glad you were concerned about me, though," he said softly.

"You . . . you . . . "

"Don't spoil it," he murmured and his fingers threaded into her hair and forced her head down towards him.

"No!" Gemma made a valiant effort to extricate herself — to heave herself away from that potent male body underneath her own.

He had no intention of giving her up so easily however. "I think you owe me something, sweet Gemma," he reasoned.

"Owe you . . . ?" Blankly she gazed down into his eyes as she strained to pull away.

His arm tightened around her waist. "I didn't know you cared," he said lightly. "Yet here you are, shedding tears over me."

Gemma dashed her hand impatiently across her eyes and in so doing came close to losing her balance yet again. He took advantage of her unsteadiness and once more she felt the urgent pressure around her, urging her down towards him. "I don't owe you anything," she blurted out.

"Not even an apology for trying to kill me?" he asked, and there was a suggestive twitch to his lips.

Gemma tried to deny the attraction she felt for Carr Winterton. She tried to bring to the fore all the doubts and fears she'd had about him. "I'm sorry then," she gasped out. "Now — please let me go."

* * *

But slowly he drew her head down and despite her little moan of protest he fastened his lips on hers. Carefully then, he rolled her over until she was beside him on the large bed. Gemma's feeble squeak of protest was overruled completely by even more pressure being brought to bear on her already bruised mouth. In the end it was easier not to oppose him, for she rapidly found that when she struggled the steely band around her waist tightened, but when she stopped it really was quite pleasant. The marauding mouth seemed attuned to her responses, too — plundering when she thrashed her head from side to side, but growing gentle again when she desisted. The hands she beat against him might as well have been frail moths fluttering against a flame for all the impact they made. In the space of minutes he had tamed her. One hard-muscled thigh pressed against the lower half of her body held her immobile, and effectively it warned her that any movement from her might be interpreted as all-out war. One last tear squeezed itself out onto her cheek and he kissed it away. She tried to convince herself she was glad her mouth had been freed, she could tell him just what she thought of him now . . . She forced her eyes open and prepared to do battle, but he was leaning over her now and the expression in those smoky-grey eyes chased away all thought of arguing. "Still want me to let you go?" he asked gently.

Gemma moved slightly. She was free to ease away now if she wanted. Even though his arm was still across her body and his lips so near, she knew instinctively that he would not hold her against her will. Her dampened lashes swept up from her cheeks. "I — I thought I'd killed you," she said wretchedly.

"It was unforgivable of me allowing you to think you had," he said.

"Unforgivable!" she agreed, but her

voice was husky and she couldn't be angry any more. Suddenly she felt as if the only place she belonged in all the world was here in his arms. It was as though she'd been running away from something for a very long time — and she knew now that it wasn't just a bank robber who had temporarily thrust his way into her life she was running from. That man had nothing in common with Carr Winterton anyway. Her mind had played tricks. Carr was no armed robber. She'd never have allowed herself to fall in love with a thief . . . Love! It was the first time she'd admitted to the word, but suddenly Gemma knew the truth. It was what was happening to her. It was what she'd been fighting against all this time. But how could she have allowed such a thing to happen after Keith's bitter betrayal?

"I'm sorry," Carr said. "You really were upset, weren't you?"

"Upset!" Gemma tried to laugh but failed miserably in the attempt.

"Upset . . . " Her voice wavered. "I was devastated! I never believed in my wildest dreams that I could pull a gun on someone — much less shoot them."

"They're nasty little playthings," he agreed.

"I'll never touch one again." She shuddered. "Not even that stage one," she vowed with determination.

"Yes, you will." There was a firm note in his voice.

Gemma's response was swift. "No! I won't . . . "

"I'm going to show you how to use one," he said.

"I couldn't . . . " Her eyes widened in horror.

He eased away from her slightly and the movement freed her completely. Then he leaned above her and watched her as she lay beside him. "Gemma, my sweet," he argued patiently. "It might be as well if you knew what to do in an emergency."

"Don't . . . " she pleaded.

"You were waving the damn thing in the air like it was a flag," he persisted. "Nobody would be scared of you, handling it like that."

"I don't *want* anybody to be scared of me." The finality of her tone left no room for doubt.

Carr pushed himself up from the bed and crossed to the other side of the room. When he returned she saw he had retrieved Tess's weapon from the floor. Unwillingly she shuffled herself to a sitting position and stared at him, hugging her knees up under her chin.

"Come on," he said, and smiled down reassuringly.

"Where to?" Fiercely Gemma determined to hold onto her resolve and have nothing more to do with firearms.

"I'll show you how to bluff."

Gemma scowled. "I thought you didn't agree with violence," she retorted.

"We're in a dicey situation, you and me."

"No! It's me who's in the situation,

232

Carr," she said reasonably. "You never saw the man."

"He'll have to get at me before he does you," Carr replied.

Fear leaped inside her. "It mustn't come to that . . . " Reluctantly she slid off the bed and stood before him, agitated and uncertain.

"Maybe it won't," he said. "But no harm will be done by your learning how this thing would work if it *were* a real one."

Still hesitant, Gemma stood her ground. "All right," she agreed. "You can show me, but don't expect me to fire it again, will you?"

"Come over here." Without anticipating any further argument, Carr walked over to the window. Once there he swung round to face her.

"Why?" Still she was unwilling.

"Because you need the length of the room to focus on something," he said with infinite patience.

"I won't fire it!"

"I know! I know!"

Averse to even touching the weapon again, Gemma went slowly towards him. "Good girl!" He subjected her to a cool look of appraisal, then went on in the most reasonable way possible, "Gemma my sweet, just imagine that doorpost over there is wearing a balaclava mask, will you? Imagine, too, that it's pointing a nine-millimetre Beretta at your head."

"Is that what this gun is?" she asked, mildly interested.

"It's a clever copy," he said. "It could just as easily be a sawn-off shotgun that the doorpost is holding though, or a Colt or a . . . "

"Okay! Don't confuse me." Gemma frowned. "So — what do I do?"

Carr explained in detail, showing her how the magazine was loaded. "First, you apply the safety — though I confess, I hadn't done that," he said with a grim little laugh. "You then have fifteen shots in a full magazine," he continued, and held out the weapon for her to take from his hand.

Gemma shivered but did not recoil. She weighed the gun tentatively in her hand. "It's so heavy," she said, subdued. "That's what made me think it was the real thing."

"You'll need two hands," he pointed out and promptly turned her round by the shoulders to face the door. Quietly, behind her then, he described how she should stand. "Feet apart," he ordered, and then both his arms reached round her body and clasped over her wrists. He positioned her hands on the pistol, lifting it up to eye-level. His voice was soft against her ear. "This is the rear sight," he explained, pointing to a projection just above the hammer. "This is the front sight." His fingers slid along the barrel. "You must line up the front one with the centre of the rear sight, okay?"

Gemma peered along the line of the gun. "Hey that's clever." She focused on the doorpost.

"It will kick back," he warned. "And hard! So be prepared."

"I know!" She grimaced.

"But you'll allow for that," he said. "You'll aim deliberately just a slight way off target. With this one it's roughly three inches, I'd guess."

"Higher, lower or sideways?"

"Lower!"

"So — I'd hold it — just above — there!" Gemma lowered the barrel slightly.

"Depends whether you want to shoot him through the head or the heart."

"Straight through the heart," she answered with spirit.

"Then a bit higher, my sweet," Carr retorted with a laugh.

"How do you know where a doorpost's heart is?"

Carr gave a sigh of resignation. "I'm assuming that he's six feet four or thereabouts," he said. "Therefore his heart will be at about five-eight."

"I never thought of that." Gemma nodded thoughtfully.

"Your hands will be straight out in front of you." Carr adjusted her stance slightly, his own arms still encircling her.

Gemma liked the feel of those arms around her. She experienced a thrill of pleasure as his hard body pressed against her spine. "Like this?" She adopted a rigid stance.

"Relax!" he said. "And breathe — in first, then out again as you squeeze the trigger."

"I'm not going to shoot . . . it still smells like the bonfire parties I went to as a kid, in here." She sniffed the air disapprovingly.

"The safety's on," Carr assured her.

"But I know what to do now." She half turned towards him, a ready smile on her lips.

"Yes, you know what to do," he said softly. "But I couldn't resist keeping my arms around you that little bit longer." His eyes locked with the dancing, cat-green ones of the girl he held.

"I — I think I should go down and make a meal . . . " She lowered her eyes.

Carr took the gun from her and tossed it onto the bed. "I'll come too," he said. "I don't want you left alone for even a minute — we're too close to moving out of here to risk anything now."

"Do you think he's heard the shots?"

Carr nodded. "Unless he's stone-deaf — yes!"

"I'm sorry . . . "

"It's done now." He smiled and brushed her cheek gently with the knuckles of one hand. "Don't look so worried."

"But you warned me . . . " Apprehensively she bit on her lip. "Now it will be my fault if something goes wrong."

"Look, love," Carr took her firmly by the shoulders and made her look at him. "The only thing that's happened is that whoever is out there will now know we have a gun. What he doesn't know is that it's a fake, so maybe you've done us both a favour by broadcasting the fact that we're prepared for him."

"Do you think so?" Worriedly she gazed up at him.

Firmly he turned her towards the door. "At least," he said kindly, "you seem to be trusting me now, so I'll forgive you for giving the real villain something to think about."

"Carr . . . " Hesitantly she paused as they reached the passageway outside.

"What is it, sweetheart?"

Gemma's heart lurched at the easy endearment. "About — about that other gun . . . "

"The other one?" Obviously he had no idea what she was talking about.

"The one the man had — when he held me up." Uneasily she looked down at the floor, unable to meet his gaze.

"Yes?" His expression cleared. "What about it?"

"You knew what type it was," she rushed on. "It's what made me suspicious of you. Carr . . . how *did* you know, when even Inspector Franklyn didn't?"

"I don't know what kind it was, Gemma," Carr said with a shrug. "Whatever gave you the idea that I did?"

"You said . . . " Gemma paused and screwed up her forehead as she sought to remember his exact words. "You said something about a point four five government issue."

"Did I?" He frowned in concentration, then his face broke into a grin. "Yes — now I remember. I did, didn't I?" He reached out one hand and curled it around hers. "Just a wild guess, Gemma. You see, I'd just finished a story where I'd mentioned one of those. It must still have been in my mind."

It was an easy explanation. But couldn't it just be *too* easy, Gemma wondered. Immediately she scolded herself for being over-cautious. "I see!" She smiled brightly but somehow seemed to withdraw from him.

"Gemma?" Suddenly his face was incredulous. "Surely you're not saying that you've suspected me all along just because of that?"

"You did say it," she insisted.

"I remember now," he said. "But I've no idea what kind of guns were used in the raid. It was just a figure of speech — a wild guess. They could have used any one of a dozen kinds."

He seemed so open, so honest, that all of a sudden Gemma felt ashamed of her misgivings. "I'm sorry, too," she muttered, averting her eyes again.

She watched him as he ran easily down the stairs. At the bottom, he turned to her and there was strain in his face. "Look," he said. "I can't stand any more of this cloak-and-dagger stuff — and you going all scared on me again. I'm going to fetch the car now and get you to safety."

"No, Carr . . . it might not be safe out there." Gemma flung herself down the staircase to his side.

"Drop the catch on the door while I'm gone," he ordered, and there was a grim set to his lips and no laughter in those steady grey eyes.

"Please . . . Carr — let's wait until it's dark," she pleaded. "You did say . . . "

"I think I've said far too much in the past," he broke in. "You take every word I've uttered and turn it round and inside out to try and prove to yourself I'm the bad guy."

"I don't believe that now." She reached out and touched his arm.

"While ever we're here together there'll always be a doubt in your mind," he said.

Gemma shook her head, tears threatening. "I want to trust you . . . "

He shrugged. "So maybe you will when I hand you in at police headquarters," he informed her.

"Do we have far to go?" she wanted to know.

"No more than five miles as the crow flies," he said with a short little laugh. "But nearer ten by road — the conventional way. Now — remember what I said — drop the catch on the door. Give me five minutes and I'll be back. Okay?"

Numbly she nodded. "I'll need my jacket . . . and a change of shoes." Gemma gazed down at the soft slippers Tess had provided.

"You'll have time to pop upstairs and get the coat," he said kindly. "But lock the door first. Understand?"

Gemma nodded. Her hand fell away from his arm. He smiled down at her. "I *do* understand," he said, then cautiously he opened the door a crack and peered outside. "But Gemma, love — I'm not the most patient or the most understanding of men, I guess."

"Yes, you are," she said miserably. "It's me who's to blame — I'm too wary of men."

"We won't argue about that now," he replied and with the words slipped through the door. "Close it," he ordered. "Immediately! And don't forget . . . "

"The catch," Gemma finished for him with a little smile.

She closed the door and clicked the

lock into place, then swiftly she ran back up the stairs. Once in her bedroom Gemma lost no time in slipping on the sensible building society shoes and it was as she rummaged in her wardrobe that she heard the creak of a stair . . .

* * *

Carr couldn't have come back inside, she reasoned. She hadn't heard the car engine starting up anyway. More than a little apprehensively, she dropped her jacket on the bed and crept stealthily to the door. She crept out onto the little landing. A figure was silhouetted at the top of the stairs. She couldn't make out his face because the sun was too bright behind him. But he was tall. His fair-blond hair made a halo above a grey jacket. Something glinted in his hand; it was *not* the Beretta replica — this gun was smaller, the kind that could easily be slipped into a pocket . . .

Gemma heard a scream and realized it was her own. Then, reason returned and she fled along the passage towards the bathroom — the only room, she remembered, that had a bolt on its inside. Panting, she leaned back against the door once she'd pushed the bolt home to lock it. Frantically her eyes swept the tiny room, searching for a hiding-place, but she knew there was none. Gemma raced over to the window and began to wrench at it, but it was jammed solid by years of paint sticking to its hinges. Behind her a shot rang out and she jerked round in time to see the wooden door splintering. Instinctively she made a dive for the great iron bathtub and huddled down inside it as the gun was fired several times more. She felt the bath shuddering as metal hit it below its rim. By now she was sobbing and terrified. In another few seconds he'd managed to shoot the lock away, she knew. She peeped over the edge of the bath and saw the whole doorframe loosening as a heavy shoulder was thrust against the stout oak panels of the door itself. Slowly the bolt began to give way and then the door was swinging inwards.

* * *

Another shot rang out, but this time it sounded as if it came from the direction of the passage outside. Gemma buried her face in her hands. The time for tears was past. She closed her eyes tightly. If the gunman was Carr Winterton, then she didn't want to know. It was better he should shoot her here, like this, than she should look in his eyes and learn the truth. She was deathly cold and fear like she'd never known before had her in its grip. She waited, agonized, for the pain to rip through her body, her head, her limbs. Where would he aim the gun for the greatest effect, she wondered dully.

* * *

But nothing happened, and now there was no sound save a scuffling in the passage outside. Still Gemma dared not move. It could be a trick. She heard the distant sound of breaking glass, and then footsteps — the urgent creak of several stairs as if someone was coming up them in a hurry. And then she heard his voice yelling, "Gemma! Gemma! For God's sake where are you?" The door crashed open and then rough hands were hauling her out of the bathtub. When she dared look at him, she saw that his face was stricken and white. "Gemma!" The way he said her name in that disturbed and husky tone brought some warmth back into her, but even so her legs felt so weak that had it not been for his support Gemma would have crumpled at his feet. "Are you hurt?" he demanded and when she tried to answer and couldn't he shook her impatiently. "Gemma! Speak to me," he ordered. "Did he get you with any of the shots?" His eyes were tortured and he was running his hands over her now, turning her round gently, smoothing back her hair as he brought her round to face him again. "Did he knock you into the bath, sweetheart? Did you lose consciousness? Oh, god — Gemma — say something. You're in shock, I know, but what the hell did that monster do?"

She shook her head and managed a hoarse whisper. "I'm all right, Carr . . . I'm not hurt . . . "

"You're not? You're sure?" Less frantic now, he stared at her, wanting desperately to believe her, she knew, but still not convinced there wasn't a bullet-hole somewhere in her.

"I — I jumped in the bath," she said weakly. "There was nowhere to hide — it was all I could think of . . . he was shooting through the woodwork."

Carr pulled her into his arms and rocked her gently against his body. "Thank God for the old bathtub," he murmured.

"How did he get in . . . ?" Gemma clung onto the rock-like stability of Carr Winterton's shoulders.

"He forced a window in the

study — that was the way he went out again, too — except that he took most of the glass with him that time. He must have broken in while we were up here."

"Where is he now?" Her gaze went beyond him, fearfully searching the corridor of the little house.

"He must have heard me coming up the stairs," Carr said. "He knocked me out of the way and took a shot at me."

"You're . . . you're not . . . ?"

"He missed!" Carr said with a grim smile. "I daren't risk following him after that — I could only think of you." He looked down at her tenderly. "I still can't believe you're all right . . . I never should have left you . . . "

"We have to get away, Carr. He'll come back." Reason was returning, together with the life to her limbs.

"We'll have to make it on foot," Carr replied savagely. "The bastard sent my car into the lake before breaking in here."

"Oh, no!" Gemma stared at him, her eyes wide and frightened.

"I rushed back as soon as I saw it," he said, then gave a dubious little grin. "The front door needs a new lock now," he said. "I just burst straight through it."

"We should go — and quickly," Gemma urged.

"Across country? Dare you risk it, Gemma?"

"We don't have much choice, do we?"

"I was hoping John would have sent somebody by now," he divulged. "He knew I was bringing you here. Tess did too."

"Tess?" Gemma frowned.

"Tess and John Franklyn are married, sweetheart."

Gemma was taken aback. "Oh! I never guessed — I thought . . . Oh, Carr, I've been such a fool."

"I told you Tess was Debra's sister — I also told you John was my brother-in-law," he said.

"I was too busy branding you the killer to add two and two and make four," Gemma confessed.

"We're wasting time!" Carr frowned and glanced at his watch. "Look, love, it's only half past four but I don't think we dare wait until it's completely dark out there. I want you to put on your warmest clothing, okay? Comfortable walking-shoes, too."

Gemma was nodding. "I can be ready in minutes, Carr."

"The only alternative is to hole up in the cellar and hope that they send somebody in time . . . "

"No, Carr — I'm not going to be forced into a corner again." Gemma was adamant.

"I'm going to pick the gun up from my room," he told her, holding her away from him. "It won't be much good, I'll admit, but it might just attract somebody's attention if we have to fire it."

He took her out of the cramped little bathroom and at the door of her bedroom released her hand. "Warm clothing," he reminded her. "Several layers, Gemma — it's going to be freezing out there tonight and we might have to lie low."

"I'll remember!" Already she was halfway through the door.

★ ★ ★

They made their way stealthily out of the back of the house, and once free of it Carr urged her to keep down low behind stone walls that divided off a mosaic of green fields. For twenty minutes or so, progress was agonizingly slow in the shelter of those ancient walls. But after a while the landscape became more open and rugged, and out in the open where they were subjected to extremes of weather some of the walls had fallen away altogether. Before them then lay fells with scarcely anywhere to take shelter. Suddenly Gemma was scared. "There's nowhere to take cover," she said, beginning to panic.

"But there's hardly any daylight left," Carr reasoned patiently. "Nobody will be able to see us, sweetheart."

"You said it wasn't far," she wailed.

"Five miles at the most," he reassured her. "Possibly less to the nearest village."

"*Possibly?* Don't you know *exactly?*"

He squeezed her hand which he'd held all the way so far. "I don't make a habit of walking into Craigmere for my groceries," he joked. "Usually it's more convenient to take the car."

Instantly Gemma felt remorse for bickering over so trivial a matter. "I'm sorry about your car." Suddenly the thought of the danger they were in came back to her. "Is it a complete write-off?"

He grinned. "I wouldn't think so. It had just taken a slight nose-dive into the shallows."

"Is this really the right way we're going?"

"I hope so!" Carr's hand tightened

round hers once more as she stumbled in the almost pitch darkness. "It's a pity there's no moon tonight."

Nervously, Gemma glanced behind. "I — I thought I heard something . . . "

"Probably nightbirds," he said cheerfully. "There'll be animals, too — foxes and rabbits."

"I'm scared, Carr . . . " She hurried to keep up with his long, easy strides.

"So am I, sweetheart," he teased. "I told you before, I'm not the heroic type."

"You rushed into the house to save me."

"A spontaneous reaction," he said, making light of the whole affair. "Look," he changed the subject, "see over there, Gemma — it must be the Penrith to Carlisle motorway."

Gemma could see headlights flashing along a thin strip of road in the far distance. In between them and the road though she could see something else, too. "Rooftops, too," she cried, elated. "And a church spire — see? Is that Craigmere, Carr?"

"I guess so." He pulled her to a halt and even in the darkness she could tell that he was smiling. "It's no more than half a mile, Gemma . . . "

"We've made it . . . "

A shot rang out in the black void behind them. Carr hurled her to the ground and covered her with his body. "Keep still," he muttered.

"We should make a run for it," she whimpered helplessly.

"It's too far," he said against her ear.

"He's going to kill us . . . "

"Keep calm," he ordered softly. "I'll hold him off while you make a dash for it."

"No! I'm not leaving you," Gemma said, dismayed.

"This isn't the time to be a martyr," he rasped, and with the words he eased away from her. "Keep low," he commanded. "If necessary, crawl along the ground."

"I can't leave you . . . "

"You *can*, Gemma. You've got to do this — for both of us."

★ ★ ★

Another explosion ripped through the night air. Gemma heard the zing of a bullet grazing off a boulder nearby. "Okay!" Carr said with determination. "Let's show the bastard two can play at this game."

Gemma caught sight of a glint of steel in his hand. He turned away from her, crouching low in the coarse grass. She pressed both hands to her ears and bit hard on her lip as Carr pulled the trigger. The sound of the return gunfire seemed to have the desired effect.

"Go now!" he ordered. "You can make it to the village in about ten minutes," he said quietly.

"I'm staying with you."

"Go and get help," he insisted. "We can't afford to let him get away this time."

"What will you do?" Her eyes were

wide and questioning in the darkness.

"I'll keep shooting as he gets nearer." His tone was impatient.

"But you only have twelve shots left," she panicked.

He turned to grin at her. "At least you remembered *something* of what I taught you."

"Does he have fifteen too?"

"He wasted some on the bathroom door, remember?"

"But he could have spare cartridges . . . "

"Just go, Gemma — you're wasting precious time," he said.

"No . . . "

"Yes, sweetheart."

"But if you're killed . . . "

"I'm tough," he stated in a resigned tone.

Gemma wanted to hug him. "No, you're not," she said. "And I want you alive."

"You do?" He stared hard at her.

Tearfully she nodded.

"Why?"

"I want time to make up for ever doubting you," she whispered brokenly.

"I'll hold you to that." A slow smile spread over his face. "I'll expect payment in full, I'm warning you."

"Carr!" She reached out a hand to him and he grasped it tightly.

"Don't worry," he said, "I'll be around to collect my reward. Now — do as I say, Gemma." Her hand was freed. She knew it was useless to argue any more. If she stayed he'd defend her to the last. "Keep down low," he warned. "And when you've gone about fifty yards, get up and go like the wind, okay?"

"Yes." Gemma began to wriggle away through the grass. Behind her she heard rustlings, then another bullet whistled past her head. Carr returned the fire. She went more quickly but two shots in quick succession blasted out behind her. She heard a muffled thud, and daring to look behind her was alarmed that she couldn't see anything at all in the darkness.

"Carr . . . " she called softly. "Are you all right?"

There was no reply, yet she knew she had not moved far enough away to be out of earshot. She scrambled round in the long grass, crouching low, then silently she began inching back the way she had come.

She almost fell over him in the darkness. His arm was flung out to one side and he was motionless. Gemma wanted to scream and only just managed to stop herself. His face was white and there was blood on his forehead. The gun was still in his outstretched hand and without further thought she disengaged the inert fingers and took it from him. Another shot rang out, but she was pleased about that because it told her roughly where he was. She began to walk towards him. Seeing a glint in the dark ahead of her, she lifted Tess's gun and fired it. In the gloom, an outcrop of large boulders had hidden him until then. Now, accustomed to the night, Gemma saw the shape of a man dart out. She fired the gun again. He whirled to face her and lifted his own weapon and she was barely six feet away from him. Swiftly she hurled the gun at his head. He yelled in pain and his own gun clattered over the rocky ground. Almost immediately he threw himself after it, but Gemma had seen her opportunity. She was lighter on her feet and she reached the gun first. Crouched then, and with her arms fully extended in front of her, she levelled it at his body.

"Lady, you just wouldn't dare," he drawled.

"Try me!" Gemma's voice was devoid of emotion.

A pale moon soared out as clouds sped across the night sky. She gasped, for the resemblance the man bore to Carr Winterton was uncanny. These grey eyes though were cold, and this face was lean and moody. His hair, though the right colour, was longer than Carr's and it needed a good grooming. The height of both men was roughly the same, however, and Gemma could understand now why she'd been suspicious of Carr.

He brought one hand up from his side and she was aware that he had Tess's gun in it. "So — who's the fastest shot?" he leered as he pointed it at her head.

Gemma swallowed hard and wondered if she'd be able to shoot him so cold-bloodedly. He didn't know the gun he was holding was a fake, she reasoned, so it would be like her shooting an unarmed opponent. It would be called murder! Her mind shied away from violence . . . And then she thought of Carr, lying bleeding back there in the darkness, and she knew she *could* kill this man if she had to.

11

SHE saw his hand tighten on the gun. Gemma steeled herself for the explosion, but jumped all the same when it came. When she didn't fall to the ground, either lifeless or screaming, he looked absurdly surprised. Then his face darkened as he realized he'd been fooled. "You bitch," he ground out through clenched teeth. "You bloody, wily bitch!"

He lunged towards her and Gemma took careful aim. He came down in a heap, almost at her feet, howling with the agony of a bullet through his foot. He rolled over and over and Gemma backed away shaking. She felt physically sick with horror at the thought of what she'd done. She wished the man would stop screaming . . . She lifted her hands to cover her ears . . .

A pair of strong arms grasped her

from behind and Gemma fought like a wildcat. "Easy! Easy, Mrs Brent," came a voice she knew. Instantly, she went limp and the man turned her round to face him. Others were there, too, several of them surrounding the man she'd shot. Pin-pricks of light dotted the landscape and a white police Range-rover was bumping over the rough ground behind him, lights full on.

"Inspector Franklyn!" She stared at him.

"Just in time, I think." He smiled down at her. "May I have the gun?" He held out his hand.

"I — I shot him . . . " she gasped.

John Franklyn stared cold-eyed at the man they were carrying towards the Range-rover. "He'll live," he stated without concern.

"Carr . . . " Her eyes sought the gloom. "Carr . . . he's . . . "

"He's been hurt. I don't know how seriously, Mrs Brent. They're taking him away now."

"He . . . he wasn't . . . "

He shook his head. "No! Don't worry. There was still a good pulse."

"I have to go to him . . . "

"Of course. I'll take you to the hospital myself." Gently he began to lead her away. The Range-rover was speeding off towards the village, blue light flashing. "There's a track to a farm just a hundred yards away," he explained. "Someone heard the first shot and luckily rang the police."

"You were quick!"

"We were already on our way. We'd found the car in the lake at Black Gill," he explained.

* * *

It was two hours before they allowed her to see Carr. He was pale and bandaged but at least he was sitting up in a hospital bed and able to talk.

"They say I have to stay for twenty-four hours," he protested.

Gemma clasped his hand. "You

were unconscious, Carr — it's to be expected."

"I let you down, sweetheart."

"You were shot," Gemma said. "I didn't expect you to be my knight in shining armour with a bullet in your head."

"Hardly that!" He grimaced. "Just a graze really but it knocked me sideways onto a rock."

"At least you're all right now . . . "

"John said you'd been worried."

Gemma laughed a little shakily. "Worried!" She'd been out of her mind until she'd known he was in no danger.

"Care to look after the invalid for a while?"

"You, Carr?" She gazed at him and he squeezed her fingers hard.

"Well, I'm not referring to that guy you put a bullet through, sweetheart."

She shuddered. "Don't remind me."

"He would have done the same to you," he said steadily. "Gemma — when I even start to think of what could have happened . . . "

"It didn't," she reassured him.

"So — what's your answer?"

"To looking after the invalid?"

"Yes!" He rested his head back on the pillows and the little smile she'd grown to love played about his lips.

"Surely you don't expect me to come and live in your back-of-beyond little house?" she said.

"I'd like you to."

"B-but I have a job waiting for me — back in Abbeykirk . . . "

"Do you want me to go down on one knee?"

Gemma looked at him solemnly. "It's a draughty old place, with no electricity and no telephone," she hedged.

"No lock on the door either — now," he said. "And my car is still in the lake. There's not much to endear the place to you, is there?"

"Except you," Gemma said in a determined manner.

"I'll have the whole place modernized — if that's what you want."

She shook her head, smiling. "It isn't, Carr."

"Well, a new bathroom at least," he promised.

"Don't you dare get rid of my piebald lion," Gemma challenged. "He saved my life, I'll have you know."

"But the enamel's all discoloured."

"We'll have it done over."

"And the door is shot to pieces."

"The door *can* be replaced," she allowed.

"Does this mean your answer is yes?" he asked softly.

Gemma's eyes were soft with love. "We don't really know each other very well, do we?"

"That can soon be remedied," Carr said as he leaned up to touch his lips to hers.

She nodded. "I'd like that."

"We'll get to know each other while we do the old place up, shall we?" he said.

"You really do have a cheek," Gemma retorted. "What do you expect me to do? Dig the garden? Scrub the floors?"

He kissed her again, more tenderly than before. "Marry me, Gemma," he said in all seriousness. "If you don't say yes, I'll be forced to sell my little house and settle in Abbeykirk so I can keep an eye on you — and win you over."

She gazed at him. "You'd do that?"

"I've got used to having you around," he said, laughing. "I've got used to us fighting and arguing . . . "

"And taking care of me," she broke in.

"I didn't do that in the end, love. I told you I wasn't the stuff heroes are made of."

"To me you are," she said softly.

"So — will you think about what I've said?"

"Do I get a choice of bedrooms again?" Her eyes twinkled.

"Just for as long as it takes," he promised.

"Maybe it won't take long, Carr . . . "

He took both her hands in his own

and pulled her towards him. "Do you know," he said gently as he prepared to kiss her again, "somehow I have the same kind of feeling, too."

THE END

Other titles in the Linford Romance Library:

A YOUNG MAN'S FANCY
Nancy Bell

Six people get together for reasons of their own, and the result is one of misunderstanding, suspicion and mounting tension.

THE WISDOM OF LOVE
Janey Blair

Barbie meets Louis and receives flattering proposals, but her reawakened affection for Jonah develops into an overwhelming passion.

MIRAGE IN THE MOONLIGHT
Mandy Brown

En route to an island to be secretary to a multi-millionaire, Heather's stubborn loyalty to her former flatmate plunges her into a grim hazard.

WITH SOMEBODY ELSE
Theresa Charles

Rosamond sets off for Cornwall with Hugo to meet his family, blissfully unaware of the shocks in store for her.

A SUMMER FOR STRANGERS
Claire Hamilton

Because she had lost her job, her flat and she had no money, Tabitha agreed to pose as Adam's future wife although she believed the scheme to be deceitful and cruel.

VILLA OF SINGING WATER
Angela Petron

The disquieting incidents that occurred at the Vatican and the Colosseum did not trouble Jan at first, but then they became increasingly unpleasant and alarming.

DOCTOR NAPIER'S NURSE
Pauline Ash

When cousins Midge and Derry are entered as probationer nurses on the same day but at different hospitals they agree to exchange identities.

A GIRL LIKE JULIE
Louise Ellis

Caroline absolutely adored Hugh Barrington, but then Julie Crane came into their lives. Julie was the kind of girl who attracts men without even trying.

COUNTRY DOCTOR
Paula Lindsay

When Evan Richmond bought a practice in a remote country village he did not realise that a casual encounter would lead to the loss of his heart.

ENCORE
Helga Moray

Craig and Janet realise that their true happiness lies with each other, but it is only under traumatic circumstances that they can be reunited.

NICOLETTE
Ivy Preston

When Grant Alston came back into her life, Nicolette was faced with a dilemma. Should she follow the path of duty or the path of love?

THE GOLDEN PUMA
Margaret Way

Catherine's time was spent looking after her father's Queensland farm. But what life was there without David, who wasn't interested in her?

HOSPITAL BY THE LAKE
Anne Durham

Nurse Marguerite Ingleby was always ready to become personally involved with her patients, to the despair of Brian Field, the Senior Surgical Registrar, who loved her.

VALLEY OF CONFLICT
David Farrell

Isolated in a hostel in the French Alps, Ann Russell sees her fiancé being seduced by a young girl. Then comes the avalanche that imperils their lives.

NURSE'S CHOICE
Peggy Gaddis

A proposal of marriage from the incredibly handsome and wealthy Reagan was enough to upset any girl — and Brooke Martin was no exception.

A DANGEROUS MAN
Anne Goring

Photographer Polly Burton was on safari in Mombasa when she met enigmatic Leon Hammond. But unpredictability was the name of the game where Leon was concerned.

PRECIOUS INHERITANCE
Joan Moules

Karen's new life working for an authoress took her from Sussex to a foreign airstrip and a kidnapping; to a real life adventure as gripping as any in the books she typed.

VISION OF LOVE
Grace Richmond

When Kathy takes over the rundown country kennels she finds Alec Stinton, a local vet, very helpful. But their friendship arouses bitter jealousy and a tragedy seems inevitable.

CRUSADING NURSE
Jane Converse

It was handsome Dr. Corbett who opened Nurse Susan Leighton's eyes and who set her off on a lonely crusade against some powerful enemies and a shattering struggle against the man she loved.

WILD ENCHANTMENT
Christina Green

Rowan's agreeable new boss had a dream of creating a famous perfume using her precious Silverstar, but Rowan's plans were very different.

DESERT ROMANCE
Irene Ord

Sally agrees to take her sister Pam's place as La Chartreuse the dancer, but she finds out there is more to it than dyeing her hair red and looking like her sister.

HEART OF ICE
Marie Sidney

How was January to know that not only would the warmth of the Swiss people thaw out her frozen heart, but that she too would play her part in helping someone to live again?

LUCKY IN LOVE
Margaret Wood

Companion-secretary to wealthy gambler Laura Duxford, who lived in Monaco, seemed to Melanie a fabulous job. Especially as Melanie had already lost her heart to Laura's son, Julian.

NURSE TO PRINCESS JASMINE
Lilian Woodward

Nick's surgeon brother, Tom, performs an operation on an Arabian princess, and she invites Tom, Nick and his fiancé to Omander, where a web of deceit and intrigue closes about them.

THE WAYWARD HEART
Eileen Barry

Disaster-prone Katherine's nickname was "Kate Calamity", but her boss went too far with an outrageous proposal, which because of her latest disaster, she could not refuse.

FOUR WEEKS IN WINTER
Jane Donnelly

Tessa wasn't looking forward to meeting Paul Mellor again — she had made a fool of herself over him once before. But was Orme Jared's solution to her problem likely to be the right one?

SURGERY BY THE SEA
Sheila Douglas

Medical student Meg hadn't really wanted to go and work with a G.P. on the Welsh coast although the job had its compensations. But Owen Roberts was certainly not one of them!

HEAVEN IS HIGH
Anne Hampson

The new heir to the Manor of Marbeck had been found. But it was rather unfortunate that when he arrived unexpectedly he found an uninvited guest, complete with stetson and high boots.

LOVE WILL COME
Sarah Devon

June Baker's boss was not really her idea of her ideal man, but when she went from third typist to boss's secretary overnight she began to change her mind.

ESCAPE TO ROMANCE
Kay Winchester

Oliver and Jean first met on Swale Island. They were both trying to begin their lives afresh, but neither had bargained for complications from the past.

CASTLE IN THE SUN
Cora Mayne

Emma's invalid sister, Kym, needed a warm climate, and Emma jumped at the chance of a job on a Mediterranean island. But Emma soon finds that intrigues and hazards lurk on the sunlit isle.

BEWARE OF LOVE
Kay Winchester

Carol Brampton resumes her nursing career when her family is killed in a car accident. With Dr. Patrick Farrell she begins to pick up the pieces of her life, but is bitterly hurt when insinuations are made about her to Patrick.

DARLING REBEL
Sarah Devon

When Jason Farradale's secretary met with an accident, her glamorous stand-in was quite unable to deal with one problem in particular.

THE PRICE OF PARADISE
Jane Arbor

It was a shock to Fern to meet her estranged husband on an island in the middle of the Indian Ocean, but to discover that her father had engineered it puzzled Fern. What did he hope to achieve?

DOCTOR IN PLASTER
Lisa Cooper

When Dr. Scott Sutcliffe is injured, Nurse Caroline Hurst has to cope with a very demanding private case. But when she realises her exasperating patient has stolen her heart, how can Caroline possibly stay?

A TOUCH OF HONEY
Lucy Gillen

Before she took the job as secretary to author Robert Dean, Cadie had heard how charming he was, but that wasn't her first impression at all.

ROMANTIC LEGACY
Cora Mayne

As kennelmaid to the Armstrongs, Ann Brown, had no idea that she would become the central figure in a web of mystery and intrigue.

THE RELENTLESS TIDE
Jill Murray

Steve Palmer shared Nurse Marie Blane's love of the sea and small boats. Marie's other passion was her step-brother. But when danger threatened who should she turn to — her step-brother or the man who stirred emotions in her heart?

ROMANCE IN NORWAY
Cora Mayne

Nancy Crawford hopes that her visit to Norway will help her to start life again. She certainly finds many surprises there, including unexpected happiness.